Extreme Desire
And 11 other original sensual stories

By Kat Cox

Published by
Magenta & Blue

https://magentaandblue.com

Cover Illustration by
Magenta & Blue / Irene Ruiz

Magenta & Blue is a division of Dialect-Line Experiences, LLC
©2022 Magenta & Blue / Dialect-Line Expectations, LLC

Contents

Contents 3
A New Toy 5
A Very Bad Boy 17
Delayed Flight 234 27
Extreme Desire 51
Just a Crush 59
May September 81
Milestone Birthday 99
MMF 105
Under the Mimosa Tree 119
A Flat Tire in the Rain 131
Added Value 139
Shopping 149

A New Toy

I watched the tracking for the package from the minute I ordered it. When it arrived on the porch, the thud from the UPS guy as he dropped it against the door, my heart skipped a beat. It was as discreet as they'd said it would be -- no return address blaring their brand name, no packaging declaring "THIS IS A SEX TOY!" for the suburban neighborhood to see. Just a small brown cardboard box. It could be shoes. It could be a part for my husband's Dodge Ram. It could be a chew toy for the dog or a set of onesies for our six-month-old son.

But it wasn't any of these unassuming things; it was a purple vibrating anal plug, recommended by my friend Rachael at a happy hour two weeks previous.

"Oh my god," she'd exclaimed, "this thing is my absolute favorite--" and showed us pictures of it on the website where it was for sale. I had no experience with anything anal. I'd always been curious but once I got married, it felt like asking would have been too much, especially after our first child was born and we barely had time to look at each other anymore, let alone engage in new and exciting sex acts.

But Rachael insisted. She and her husband had three kids and they had a very healthy sex life, somehow. Sure, they were also polyamorous and she bragged constantly to our girls' group about her new paramour every few months. I wasn't going to try any of that. (Although she assured us all it was an open invitation to discuss if we were ever interested.)

I had bought the toy on a whim at 3 in the morning after breastfeeding my finicky son for more than an hour, exhausted. I'd had the presence of mind to use my special credit card set aside for birthday presents or other surprises for Dan, my husband, so at least he hadn't asked me about it. I'd almost forgotten until I saw my email the next day and started the tireless tracking process.

And now it was here. I opened the box and examined the packaging. Inside the cardboard it was very clear exactly what it was for. There was a charger included. It was soft silicone, but weighty, substantial. It had a loop grip on one end that made it look like a Teletubby, with a tapered cone going the other direction. It seemed a bit long for a butt plug, I thought.

"Don't forget the lube," Rachael had insisted, and shown us her favorite at the same shop. I looked back in the cardboard box and was glad to remember I had ordered some of my own.

I read the instructions and the care and handling messaging. I plugged the new toy in on my bedside table. Dan wouldn't be home for hours and hours. I had time to hide it away if I wanted to. Or I could leave it out for him to discover. Or I could introduce it after we put the baby to bed…

I left it charging and went back to my day. The house was a wreck, the baby hadn't been sleeping because he was teething, and both Dan and I were exhausted. I wasn't even sure he'd want to kiss me tonight, let alone try anything new and fun. But the thought excited me.

Dan brought dinner home -- a bit of a surprise. I was thrilled. Neither of us was up for cooking. He'd been working all day, and I'd been taking care of the house and the baby, both after basically an hour or two of sleep for the past three nights. And he was thoughtful enough to bring home something with vegetables and protein -- not just a pizza.

Such a good husband, I thought at the dinner table as we ate. I leaned over the baby in his highchair and kissed Dan with a long, wet French kiss. He smiled and kissed back, lingering together, enjoying each other's warmth. I wondered if he knew I was already turned on, thinking about my secret toy upstairs. I pulled away and looked in his hazel eyes. "I have a surprise for you," I told him.

"Oh?" he said.

"For later," I said, and went back to spooning oatmeal into the baby's mouth.

"Can't wait," Dan said, and took a bite from his dinner, waggling his eyebrows at me. I laughed.

He volunteered to bathe the baby tonight -- he normally did, so it wasn't a surprise -- but as he took the baby upstairs he patted me on my ass in the kitchen where I was cleaning up and said, "And then you can show me this surprise."

I waggled my eyebrows back at him and nodded.

But I was suddenly filled with anxiety. What if he didn't want to try the new toy? We'd never discussed anal before -- we'd both been raised in pretty conservative families and plain old sex had always been good enough for us. It had been months, though, maybe even closer to a year now, what with the pregnancy complications and the newborn and now the teething.

No, I thought. I was going to be brave. He could say no if he didn't want to try it. And knowing him, he'd just be thrilled that I had thought to try anything new. That would be enough. I wondered if the slinky black negligee I had would fit me. It had been big before the pregnancy. I finished the dishes and snuck upstairs to try it on.

It fit, better than it ever had, actually. And it was pretty comfy. I looked at myself in the mirror. I looked awful. My hair was in a messy ponytail, where it had been for probably a full week already. The bags under my eyes were atrocious. I looked frazzled and haggard and all the words we generally reserve to describe old witches in the woods.

I listened to Dan down the hall, splashing with the baby in the bath. I had enough time for a quick shower, I decided. I turned the water on and found my razor -- completely unused for months now --

and replaced the head on it. Might as well make this a production, I thought.

I thought I was showering fast, but I was still shaving a leg when Dan surprised me in the shower.

"Hey," he said, opening the door. I jumped a bit. He noticed me shaving and his eyes lit up, just enough for us both to notice. "Sorry," he said. "Just wanted to let you know the baby is out cold."

"Really?" I said.

"Yep," he said. "I guess a full week of not sleeping has caught up to him, too."

"Well, great," I said, although in my head I was trying to figure out how to time this. I'd have to feed him in an hour or two -- he'd wake up or my breasts would explode. Should I pump?

No, I thought, just go with the flow. Finish the shower and have sex with your husband while you can. Don't look a gift horse in the mouth.

"I'll be right out," I said.

"Take your time," Dan said, closing the shower door.

I got out and applied all the creams and lotions and perfumes that had gone neglected for so many months. I felt sexy, almost. Human, at least. I slid back into the negligee and looked at myself one last time before opening the bathroom door and walking back into our bedroom.

Dan was lying on the bed in his boxers, holding the new toy in his hands.

"So what's this?" he asked mischievously. He held it up to me and pressed the button on its hilt, which sent it into a spasm of vibrations.

"That," I said, taking a deep breath, "is an anal plug."

"An anal plug, eh," Dan said, examining it. He pressed the button again and the vibrations increased audibly.

"Yes," I said, crawling on the bed toward him. "With seven settings."

"Seven," he repeated, looking from the toy to me and back again. He pressed the button again, once, twice. It went from a faster buzzing to an oscillating vibration, from low to high and back. "Wow," he said.

"You wanna' try it?" I asked.

He waggled those eyebrows again.

"Of course I do," he said, and pulled me in on top of him for a long wet kiss. He slid his hands up my negligee and grabbed my ass -- still his favorite after a decade together -- in both hands. I felt my body responding immediately.

I slid my hand down between our chests as we kissed and found his cock in his shorts. It needed a little coaxing -- he was over 40 now and obviously exhausted -- but it was halfway hard already. I started stroking him, our mouths locked together, him moaning slightly as I stroked his balls, too.

"You smell so good," he breathed into my ear, sending goosebumps down my spine. His hands were all over me, as was his mouth. I loved when he nibbled my ears and my neck. It drove me absolutely crazy.

He paused for a moment to take off his boxers and then got back to kissing me, both of us starving for each other.

He laid on his back and had me kiss him and stroke him on top -- not our usual position. After a few minutes, he stopped me and took the toy in his hand.

"So how does this work, then?" he asked.

I reached over to the night table and grabbed the lube.

"Well, first," I said, "you lube it up."

"Of course," he said.

I squeezed the lube into my hand and rubbed it over the toy, feeling a little silly but also seductive. He watched with those eyebrows raised, smiling.

"I guess I need some, too," he said, and to my surprise, took the lube and squeezed some into his own hand, then rubbed it between his legs under his cock.

"Oh, yes," I said.

He put the lube to the side and then looked at me expectantly, his knees bent.

I moved without thinking and inserted the tip of the toy into his ass.

"Ooh," he said. "Slow, slow, slow."

I pushed lightly and he gasped.

"I'll hold it here," I said, "and you push against it when you're ready."

He nodded, his eyes closed, and pulled me onto him again to kiss me. I was poised in front of him within reach, and he stroked my clit gently with one hand while he used his other one to help guide me in pushing the toy inside of him.

He took it faster than I would have imagined he could have, moaning with pleasure as it went ever deeper. When it was up to the hilt, he opened his eyes. "Turn it on," he said.

I pushed the button for a moment and the vibration started. I could feel it through the ring where I held the toy now.

"Oh, wow," he said. His cock was rock hard. He was wriggling with pleasure, his eyes rolling back in his head, his mouth opening and closing soundlessly. I loved the power this gave me. I loved turning him on like this, especially when I had no idea I could.

"Turn it up," he told me, and I pushed the button again, sending it into a faster, harder vibration. He nodded and bit his lip. "One more," he begged. I pushed once more and could feel the vibration hard through the ring.

He still had a hand on my clit, although he was too distracted to really be doing anything with it. I let go of the toy, sure it would stay in place, and moved up so that I was straddling him. I took his cock in my hand and pulled it back and forth, as if testing its hardness. I found the lube again and poured another squirt into my hand, then used it on his cock.

"Oh, my god," he said. "That is… so… good."

He had always loved hand jobs, which was easy for me. He always told me how good I was at them. I stroked him, watching the pleasure wash over his face again and again.

"Will you ride me?" he asked after a few moments.

I was dripping wet now, so turned on by his obvious pleasure. I nodded and slid him into me.

"Play with yourself," he told me, gasping as I pulled him deeper and deeper into me.

So I did. I touched my clit, slowly at first, and rocked my hips back and forth. I could feel the vibration of the toy through his cock. It wasn't strong enough to be like a vibrator on my clit, but it did feel good. He was moaning with every thrust I made now, his eyes fully in the back of his head, his back arching slightly.

The thought of his orgasm turned me on more than anything else. I loved feeling him cum inside me -- it had always been my favorite when I felt like he completely lost control because I'd turned him on so much. Feeling him writhe beneath me like that was maybe the hottest thing I'd ever experienced. It took a surprisingly short amount of time for me to be cumming there, riding his cock, my own moans escaping my lips as I tightened around his cock and bucked against him.

"Fuck, fuck, fuck," he said, holding onto my ass and pushing into me as I came. "Oh, god," he said.

And then I knew he was cumming, too. Explosively. I could feel him roping inside of me, twice, three times, seven or eight times. Harder than he had ever cum, even when we were first married and would have sex two or three times a day sometimes.

I collapsed on top of him, reaching down to turn off the toy that was still vibrating inside of him. "Thanks," he said, laughing, catching his breath. He kissed the top of my head, my hair still wet from the shower. We panted together for a few moments.

The baby started crying over the baby monitor and we both tensed up.

"I'll get him," I said, starting to get up.

"Good," Dan said. "Cuz I've got to figure out how to get this out of me." We both laughed.

I went to the bathroom to pee quickly. I put a robe on over the negligee and went to kiss Dan before I headed into the baby's room. He took a deep kiss and breathed, "Thank you."

I smiled. "You're welcome," I said. "I was not expecting that."

"No?" he said, pulling back to look at me.

"No," I said, "I was not expecting you to use my new toy."

"Oh," he said, shrugging. "I thought you got it for me."

We both laughed and I kissed him again before going to take care of our child.

A Very Bad Boy

"Oh, shoot, I'm going to be late for work," Olivia said. She flew out of the bed where just a few seconds ago she'd been stroking Colby's cock while kissing him.

"But it's Sunday," Colby said, feeling the frustration settle in between his legs. It was also still dark outside -- just 6:30 in the morning, still an hour before the late autumn sun would come up.

"I took an extra shift," Olivia countered from the bathroom where he could hear her brushing her teeth. The light from over the sink was the only light in the room, and her silhouette cast a long shadow onto the bed where he lay.

He stroked himself for a moment, but the hard on was fading already. He'd finished twice the night before -- after she'd cum three times from a combination of his tongue and her vibrator -- but she was so good with her hands, he thought he could cum another five or six this morning if she'd just stay.

"The coffee shop opens before dawn on Sundays?" he said. He could hear the whine in his voice.

She spit into the sink and hung her head out the bathroom. "Yes," she said, "we open at 7:30 on Sundays."

"It's not even 7 yet," he pouted.

"Stop being such a baby," she said, a little forcefully, he thought. "You got plenty last night."

"You're going to leave me with blue balls," he said.

"Oh, come on," she said, pulling her dark hair into a high ponytail as she flew back into the bedroom and started digging in her dresser for clean clothes. "That is not a thing."

"It is," he muttered. He held the sheet over his lap, feeling pathetic as she got dressed. He supposed he should be getting dressed, too, but he really didn't want to.

"Look," she said, pulling a pair of plain white panties up to her hips and securing a neutral bra over her small breasts. "You can stay here as long as you want, ok? Sleep in a little. I'm only working until noon. They might let me go if it's slow."

He nodded, but could still feel the pout on his lips.

"If you go, though," she said, "just lock the bottom lock behind you." She threw a tee shirt over her head and grabbed her jeans from the side of the bed where they lay from the night before, shaking out the lacy, frilly pink panties she'd been wearing under them.

"I didn't see those last night," Colby said, leaning over to pick them up from where they'd fallen back to the floor.

"I think we were both a little too eager to get my pants off," she said. She was pulling on white athletic socks and slipping into a pair of slip-on shoes.

He held the panties to his nose and sniffed.

"I didn't know you were a panty sniffer," she said with a raised eyebrow.

He shrugged and dropped the panties in his lap.

"It's only been a month," he said, "I'm sure there's plenty more for you to learn about me."

She crawled up to him and gave him a deep kiss on the lips. "I hope so," she said.

She hopped back up and hurried out of the bedroom. He could hear her getting her keys out of the dish by the front door and grabbing her purse from the hook on the wall above the dish. "Be a good boy," she called as she opened the door.

"Yes ma'am," he responded as the door shut loudly behind her.

She'd left the bathroom light on, which felt a little inconsiderate for someone who had just told him to go back to sleep. He sat naked in her bed, wondering if he should jack off to her panties. He picked them back up and considered them, smelling them again. They were a rich silk, slick against his rough hands, and a blush pink with bows and frills. They were very sexy but in a good girl kind of way more than a sexy vixen kind of way, which was a surprise for Olivia. She seemed more like a black lace kind of girl. Or maybe a black leather kind of girl.

He shuddered at the thought of her in a black vinyl catsuit standing over him.

He got up to go to the bathroom and brought the panties with him, laying them on the side of the sink while he stood to pee. While he relieved himself, he noticed a frilly nighty hanging on the hook on the back of the door. He took the hem of the nighty between his fingers and felt the silky satin. It was as frilly as the panties, and he realized they were a matching set.

Without a second thought, he took the nighty off the hook and pulled it over his head. It was a little bit tight, but the satin made his nipples hard. He picked up the panties and put them on, pulling them over his half-hard cock. The satin felt smooth on his balls. He stroked his cock with a single finger and felt it hardening, too.

Colby wanted to see himself in her lingerie. Olivia had a full mirror in her tiny living room, so he walked into the living room and switched on the light.

He looked at himself in the mirror. His close cropped hair and short beard were such a contrast to the feminine frills and satin that covered his torso and his cock. The nighty was just a little too short, which showed more of the panties, which were getting more and more snug as his cock got harder and harder. He turned to look at his ass, where the pink was tight against his butt cheeks, riding up his ass crack just a little bit.

He loved it.

"Forgot my badge!" came Olivia's voice from the front door, which she was currently bursting through. She stopped in her tracks when she saw Colby standing in front of the mirror. "Oh my god," she said, her hand raising to her lips.

"Olivia," he stammered. "I can --"

"Oh my god," she said again. She let the front door close behind her, slamming shut like it always did.

He stood helplessly before her, his hands clasped in front of him. He watched in horror as she started laughing and digging in her purse.

"What are you doing?" he asked, unable to move.

She pulled her phone out and opened the camera.

"I'm sending this to the girls," she told him, snapping photo after photo of him standing pathetically before her.

"Please, no," he begged.

She laughed some more and took a few more photos, the fake camera clicking sound ringing through the living room. He noticed her laugh wasn't humorous; it was sardonic and had an angry edge.

"I cannot believe you," she said, putting her phone back in her purse and dropping the bag to the ground. In two steps she was on him, grabbing him by the ear and leading him toward the tiny breakfast room table.

"No, no," he said desperately as she sat on the hard wooden chair and pulled him down over her knee.

"You are a very, very bad boy," she said. He closed his eyes and winced in anticipation.

He could feel the force of her arm as she drew it back and brought her open hand down on his ass. The slap reverberated throughout the room.

"I can't believe you," she said again as she spanked him another time. He could feel his cheeks getting hot, both those on his face and the ones she was slapping on her thigh.

"I'm so sorry," he said. "I'll never do it again."

"It's too late for that," she said, slapping his butt cheeks again. They were stinging now as she brought her hand against him over and over.

He was completely humiliated, especially thinking about how her girlfriends would receive the photos of him. He winced at that almost as much as at the physical pain he was enduring.

"Get on the couch," she said, pushing him off her lap.

"What?" he said, stumbling to his feet.

"Get on the couch," she repeated. She was unbuttoning her jeans and taking off her shoes.

"Ok," he stammered and stepped toward the plush velvet couch a few feet away.

"What did you say?" she asked, pulling her jeans and panties down.

"Yes, ma'am," he said.

"Lay on your back," she told him. He did as she said, even though his ass was still stinging from her spanking. She stepped out of her jeans, leaving her panties in them just as she had last night.

She straddled his face.

"You dirty, dirty little boy," she said, still angry. "If you don't get me off in the next two minutes, you'll get another spanking."

He nodded, his mouth around her clit. She braced herself against the arm of the couch behind his head and started grinding against his tongue. He flicked it back and forth, slowly at first, the way he knew she liked it, and then harder and faster. After a moment he just held his tongue in place against her pussy while she rocked her hips against him, using him to stimulate herself.

He could feel the wetness of her pussy and knew her smell would be in his beard and mustache for the rest of the day. She probably wouldn't let him shower. She'd make him go to brunch with her pussy juice all over his face.

She groaned in pleasure as she came on his tongue, almost smothering him in her pleasure. He felt her clit pulsing and knew she was squeezing her pussy the same way she had on his cock the night before with her vibrator buzzing against her clit.

His cock was throbbing almost as much as his ass cheeks. The heat in his face was extremely uncomfortable, as was the tightness of the silky pink satin against his growing dick.

"You've made me late again," Olivia said, standing up and pulling her clothes back on. He stood up with her, helpless again, not knowing what to do.

"I'm so so sorry," he said. "It won't happen again."

She shook her head. "I'll be back a little bit after noon," she said, "and I want this house spotless. And you have to wear those while you clean." She pointed at the nighty and panties. "I don't care how uncomfortable it is."

"Yes ma'am," he said, shuddering in shame.

"You are not allowed to take a shower. And when I come back, you're going to fuck me," she said, taking her purse over her arm, "and you're not allowed to cum. And then you're going to buy me brunch."

He nodded.

"Such a bad boy," she said, grabbing her badge from the dish and disappearing out the door. He stood in the nighty and panties, pink with shame all over his body, as the door slammed behind her.

Delayed Flight 234

For Devin, February 14, 2021

Two hours on the tarmac. That was how long flight 234 sat before the FAA finally decided to cancel the flight for the night because of thunderstorms in St. Louis. It wasn't just the thunderstorms, of course -- it was the glut of flights that hadn't gotten out of St. Louis due to the thunderstorms.

Derrick taxied the Boeing 747 back to the gate to let the passengers off. He knew the flight attendants were going to have a hell of a group of grumpy people to deal with, including the 40 high school students who had been on the flight on their way home from a sugar-fueled week-long field trip to New York City.

But JFK wasn't such a bad airport if you had to be stuck anywhere. The airport hotel the airline would stick them in was almost luxurious, with an excellent hotel bar. Derrick knew he'd have to be up early to fly, but it wouldn't be such a bad night at this particular spot.

After all the checks were done, Derrick and his co-pilot finally caught the shuttle with the rest of the crew to the hotel and checked in for their quick, unexpected stay. Derrick tried to talk his co-pilot into having a nightcap, but Brian refused.

"I've gotta get a call in with the kiddos," he explained.

Derrick couldn't argue with this. He was kid-free, family-free, a little too free, he sometimes thought, ever since Jillian had broken off the engagement.

He knew Jillian was pregnant now, with her first child. She'd been married to another man Derrick had never heard of a quick six months after she'd ended their engagement. And now she was pregnant. He didn't know if he just hadn't been straightforward enough about wanting children himself, or if she hadn't been sexually satisfied, or what had happened. She'd just dumped him, unceremoniously, a few weeks before their wedding date, and he was left with an overpriced, highly personal engagement ring and a lot of questions.

But not tonight, he thought as he waved Brian off. Tonight he was in New York, at an airport bar, where he could pretend to be someone else, at least for a little while.

After a quick change, he bellied up to the bar and surveyed the scene. It was late -- after 11pm -- and there weren't many people drinking. Derrick didn't mind. He enjoyed sitting alone in a beautiful setting, which this bar certainly was. Old, dark wood, and brass accents. And an excellent selection of scotch.

He ordered his favorite and a snack and sat back to watch the end of a west coast basketball playoff game.

"Captain Tennyson?"

Derrick looked down from the game to a young woman's face. She was vaguely familiar but he couldn't place where he knew her from. She had golden blonde hair straightened within an inch of its life and clear skin that highlighted bright blue eyes. She had a very playful mouth, he noticed.

"Yes?"

"Fancy meeting you here!" said the woman. She had a slight southern accent. She looked at him for a moment more, waiting for him to be in on the joke, but he seemed unable to muster the recognition. "You don't recognize me at all, do you," she said dejectedly.

"I'm sorry," he said, "I don't."

"Well," she said, "we were only on the route together for a few months anyway. Janine Baker --

I was a flight attendant on the St. Louis-JFK route with you."

"Oh, yes, of course," Derrick said, although he still didn't recognize her. "Janine, how are you?"

"I'm great!" she said. "Do you mind if I sit here?"

"Oh, not at all," Derrick said, motioning to the empty barstool next to him. "I was just watching some basketball. Would you like a drink?"

"Sure!" the young woman said brightly. "Bourbon, please."

Derrick realized as she began to dig in her purse that she expected him to order for her. He signaled to the bartender and ordered a Bulleit on the rocks as Janine reapplied a sheer lip gloss.

"Thank you so much," she said. "So," she leaned in towards him and half-slouched with her hands in her lap. The move accentuated her cleavage and Derrick suddenly realized how low-cut her shirt was. "Are you still on the old route?"

"I am," Derrick said. It had actually been a few years now, he realized.

"They moved me to an international flight," Janine said, waving a thank you to the bartender as he deposited her drink before her. She took a sip. "I'm the envy of every girl back home, flying to Paris all the time now."

"Ah," Derrick said. It was a promotion to be moved to an international flight. He hadn't ever been interested in them, personally, because it meant so much time away from home. But that had been when he was planning on having a family.

"And how is your lovely wife?"

Derrick put his scotch down. He wasn't expecting that question to hit him as hard as it did.

"I don't have a wife," he stammered.

"Oh, I'm so sorry," Janine said, bringing her lovely slender hand with slick red fingernails quickly to her lips. "She didn't--? I mean-- you were engaged when -- oh no! I didn't know!"

"It's alright," Derrick said, even though it wasn't really. "She broke off the engagement. It's been a little over a year, I guess. We were never married."

"I'm so so sorry," Janine said sweetly. She put her hand on his leg, genuinely, and looked into his eyes with true concern. "That is heartbreaking."

"Yeah," Derrick said, "it was."

"Well, onward and upward," Janine said, and took up her bourbon again.

Derrick took a sip of his scotch as well and stared back at the basketball game. He hoped she hadn't noticed the color draining from his cheeks when she'd asked about his "wife".

"So are you a free agent then?" Janine asked.

"Like, am I single?" Derrick said. He nodded. "Yeah."

Hard to move on from that kind of rejection, he thought.

"Well, hurray to both of us for that then," she said.

"Indeed," he agreed. Was she hitting on him? He'd never considered having a thing for flight attendants, because he didn't like the idea of mingling work with dating, and, of course, he'd been doing everything he could to be faithful to a woman for so long. But she was definitely gorgeous and sweet and they were both single and stuck at a hotel for the night. He wouldn't kick her out of bed, he thought.

"Then we should sleep together," she said slyly, causing him to almost spit his drink out.

"Excuse me?" he said.

"Look," she said, turning to him and putting her hand back on his thigh, a bit higher this time. "You're attractive, I'm attractive, we have chemistry, and you have got to make it up to me for not remembering who I was. I have not had a good lay in months and I need someone to eat my pussy and make me cum, hard."

He couldn't believe his ears. "Okay," he said.

"And other things," she said.

He looked around to make sure someone wasn't filming this or putting it on Candid Camera. "Okay," he said again.

"Like spanking," she said. "And pulling my hair."

Derrick had never tried either of those things, but they sounded fun to him.

"And a foot rub," she said. "I need someone to worship my feet."

This hit a button in his head. He had always had a foot fetish but had kept it under wraps because his fiancée had thought it was weird.

"Worship them?" he said, swallowing hard. He glanced down at her legs now to catch a glimpse of the ankles, the arches, the toenails painted red to match her fingernails, all encased gently in a severe-looking black sandal with spike heels.

"Yes," she said, "and suck on the toes."

He didn't know if it was her directness, or what she was saying, or the fact that her fingertips were mere inches from his cock, or that it had been a while, but he knew he needed to calm down a bit before they left the bar, because he was going to be embarrassingly hard if they stood up now.

He took a drink of his Scotch and motioned for the bartender to bring the check.

"I'm in," he said.

She clapped her hands together like a happy schoolgirl. "Room 705," she said. "I'll meet you there in a bit." She kissed him on the cheek, then stood up and grabbed her purse. She left her drink and left the bar quickly, but not too fast for Derrick to miss how great her ass looked in her jeans and how hot her heels looked as she dashed away.

The bartender smirked at Derrick while he paid the bill, including the charge for a seriously overpriced and undrunk bourbon. Derrick didn't mind. He took his time finishing up, thinking about what Janine would be wearing when he met her in a few minutes. Flight attendants didn't always travel as lightly as you might expect, and lingerie was pretty light to begin with. They could fit all kinds of things into their carryon luggage, even for international flights. And if she spent time in Paris, she probably got to shop at lingerie stores he'd only ever dreamed of...

He shivered with anticipation. He was a bit of a secret lingerie connoisseur. He'd always bought fun things for his fiancée, which she'd enjoy, but she'd wear them once for him, shyly, and then put them away, never to be seen again. Sometimes he'd dig through her drawer when she was at work to take the pieces out and admire them. He never bought her the things he'd really wanted to -- the leather or bondage-looking gear. She would have hated it.

But maybe not Janine.

Derrick tried not to run through the lobby and get into the elevator. He hadn't realized how hungry he was for this kind of attention. He'd been concentrating so much on himself -- work, running, the gym, reading. Sex had been a secondary consideration, maybe even tertiary. He'd had a fling or two, but nothing fulfilling or serious. This night with Janine, he hoped, would at least be the former.

The elevator ride seemed to take forever. There were two other people in the elevator with him, a couple that couldn't keep their hands off each other. The man seemed to think Derrick couldn't see his hands on the woman's ass, grabbing away. She was trying to stifle a giggle. She kissed him, a messy wet kiss that made sloppy noises. Derrick would have found it gross if he wasn't already turned on and expecting something even better shortly. The couple got off on the fifth floor and Derrick almost started stroking himself for the last two floors, but he stopped himself.

He found room 705 easily and knocked gently on the door.

Janine answered in a robe. Derrick couldn't tell what was under it. He noticed she was still in heels, though. "Hello," she said quietly. She glanced around him, probably making sure there weren't other colleagues who could notice, then pulled him into her room and shut the door behind him.

She kissed him aggressively before he could greet her back. She tasted sweet. "What took you so long?" she said. He was thrown off, but he liked it.

"I --" he started.

She pressed a finger against his lips. "Shut up," she said.

She shrugged out of the robe to reveal a full lace catsuit hugging every inch of her skin. It was accented with 3" studded leather strips at cleverly placed intervals -- over her nipples, around her biceps, around her toned thighs, around her waist. She wore the same sandals she had worn earlier, but now he realized they were Roman-style sandals that wrapped in more black studded leather up her calves to her knees. Her blonde hair was pulled back into a severe bun. She wore bright red lipstick to match her nails, just as lacquered and slick looking.

Before he could try to speak again she had grabbed his package through his pants and held them in her hands, menacingly. She leaned in and whispered in his ear.

"Listen," she said, "you have to do every single thing I say. No questions. You get no say." Derrick nodded. "You can have one safe word. The first thing that comes to your mind. What is it?"

"Pineapple," Derrick muttered. Had he been thinking of that for a long time? It came surprisingly quickly.

"Pineapple," Janine nodded. "Ok, don't forget that." She squeezed his balls and cock tighter. He was already so hard, he didn't think he could get harder, but if she kept that up, he knew she would.

"If it gets too hard for you, that's the only word you're allowed to say other than 'yes, mistress' or 'no, mistress'. You'll be punished otherwise."

He nodded.

"What?" she said, squeezing him in her hand.

"Yes, mistress," he said quietly.

"I can't hear you," she said.

He cleared his throat and said it louder. "Yes, mistress."

"Good," she said. "Now take off all your clothes. Quickly."

He stumbled a little but slipped out of his shoes, his shirt, his jeans. He pulled his undershirt over his head and started to take off his boxers.

"Take off your socks first," Janine said.

"Yes, mistress."

He sat on the bed and pulled his socks off. When he was done, she was standing over him. She pushed him back onto the bed and straddled him. He noticed then that the lace catsuit had a slit over her pussy and ass. She started fingering her clit and dry humping his hard cock through his boxers.

"Good boy," she said. "I like how hard you are. Do you like how hard you are?"

"Yes, mistress," he said. He wanted to touch her, to feel how wet she was. She was clearly enjoying him. Her body was perfect under the lace, and he would have loved to watch her tits bounce as he thrust into her. But that wasn't happening yet.

She moaned and arched her back. He wondered if she was cumming already, but he couldn't ask her. She was probably edging. It was so hot.

After the moan passed, she stopped fingering her clit and climbed off him, standing back on the floor. "Move," she said, pointing to the head of the bed. Derrick scrambled up the bed to the pillows and started to remove his boxers.

"Absolutely not," Janine said, grabbing his ankle from the end of the bed. "Did I tell you to take your shorts off?"

"No, mistress," he said, his hands whipping away from his shorts, holding them up like he was under arrest.

"Correct," she said. "You have to leave them on."

"Yes, mistress."

"Now," she said, sitting on the edge of the bed. "I need that foot worship."

Derrick wasn't sure how he was supposed to do that exactly. He wanted to crawl on the floor, to see her standing over him. He shuddered with pleasure at the thought.

She climbed onto the bed, shoes and all, and stood over him.

"I want you to take off my shoes," she ordered, "slowly."

She pushed the sole of her right foot into his balls, steadying herself by placing her hands on the ceiling. Derrick moaned. He hadn't realized how much he wanted this.

"Oh, you like that, do you?" Janine said.

"Yes, mistress," he moaned. She pushed harder, the sole of the shoe digging into his soft balls. He could feel the sharp heel of the shoe grazing the base of his cock under his balls. It felt deliciously dangerous.

He closed his eyes and leaned his head back as he moaned.

"Bad boy," she said. "I need you to keep your eyes on me."

"Yes, mistress," he said, snapping back to attention.

She released his balls from her heel, and put the heel on his chest. "Undo the straps," she told him.

"Yes, mistress."

Derrick fumbled a little bit. The shoes had two tiny silver buckles at the top of her calf, as well as a zipper in the arch. He was throbbing under his boxers, and could still feel her shoeprint on his balls. He undid the silver buckles and started unwinding the studded leather. The straps had been tight on her skin, and he could see the red marks they'd left. This made him shudder again. He held the shoe in his hand after he had taken it off her foot.

"Smell it," she told him.

"Yes, mistress." He brought the shoe to his face. It smelled of leather and a vanilla perfume.

"Lick it," she said.

"Yes, mistress."

He ran his tongue over the heel of the shoe, the outer sole, the inner sole, relishing it.

"You little bootlicker," she cooed over him, looking down as he did his work.

"Yes, mistress," he uttered.

"Put the right shoe on the floor."

"Yes, mistress." He did so, gently, with reverence.

"Now the other one," she said. She shifted her weight to her bare right foot and rested her left foot on his chest, the heel digging in slightly.

"Yes, mistress."

He was more adept with the buckles this time, but tried not to move too fast in unwrapping the leather straps from around her calves and ankles. He wanted to kiss every part of her legs and feet now, but he dared not. He stole a glance up and could see her bare pussy peeking through the slit in the catsuit. It was glistening and wet. He wanted to taste it almost as much as he wanted to suck on her toes. Later, he thought. Soon, he hoped.

"You may lick this shoe, too," she told him as he gently pulled it off her foot. He complied, saying "yes, mistress" quickly, and she watched him intently, not smiling or scowling. She had a neutral look on her face, until she arched an eyebrow and he knew she enjoyed telling him what to do.

"And now I want that foot rub," she demanded.

"Yes, mistress," he said. He took her left foot in his capable hands and started rubbing the arch with his thumbs, hard. She gasped.

"Oh, right there," she said. "My poor feet. Harder."

He pushed harder, his cock feeling harder, too. He could still see her wet pussy, imagining it throbbing with want as he rubbed her feet. He held her foot near his face, hoping she'd notice.

"Oh, you want to use your tongue, do you?" she asked.

"Yes, mistress."

"Then you may," she said.

"Yes, mistress," he said. He took her toes in his mouth one by one, sucking them off while he pushed his thumbs deeper into her arches. She pushed against the ceiling above her and arched her back. It seemed that she was liking this almost as much as he was.

After a few moments, she collapsed onto the bed, tired of standing. "Keep going," she told him as she settled across from him on the king-size bed, her feet in his lap.

"Yes, mistress," he said, as her left foot found his balls and he started massaging her right foot. He kept using his tongue, sucking on her toes, kissing the arches, moving his hands up to her ankles.

"You want the rest of my legs?"

"Yes, mistress," he said. He started massaging her right calf through the lace, secretly fingering the red marks that had been left by the leather straps of the shoes.

"Tough," she said, and sat up. He put his hands up again, surrendering. He could rub her feet and legs and suck on her toes all night, but he had to do what she said.

"You're going to suck my clit instead," she said.

"Yes, mistress," he agreed.

But before he could get to that, she paused over his cock and pulled it out of his boxers. "You've been so bad," she said to his hard, throbbing dick. She slapped it and then grabbed his balls in her left hand. "You dirty, dirty boy," she said, still addressing his cock. She was still holding his balls in her left hand, hard, and she started stroking him with her right hand. She spit on the tip of the cock and rubbed the saliva down his shaft. Then she took the tip in her mouth while she kept stroking it, holding his balls like her hand was a vise.

He gasped and groaned as she took his whole cock into the back of her throat and sucked, hard. The noises coming from her mouth were sounds he'd only ever heard in porn before. He was afraid he might cum if she didn't stop, but he wouldn't dare say pineapple.

"You like that?" she asked, coming up for air, still stroking his cock and grabbing his balls. "You dirty boy."

"Yes, mistress," he said.

She took him back into her mouth and kept sucking. Now she was rotating her right hand around the base of his cock while she sucked, moving her mouth in a circular rotating around him as she sucked.

He started bucking his hips slightly, uncontrollably under her. He couldn't help it. He wanted to fuck her mouth, even though he knew she wouldn't let him. He tried to keep his reflexes to a minimum.

Just before he thought he would burst, she stopped sucking. She slapped his cock and balls again, both hard. "Bad boy," she said.

She sat up and climbed onto his chest. "I'm going to climb on your face now," she said.

"Yes, mistress," he said.

"And you're going to suck my clit and taste my wet pussy."

"Yes, mistress."

"You may say 'please'."

"Please," he begged.

"Good boy," she said.

She pulled her thighs over each side of his head and settled her pussy over his open mouth. She held apart the lace so that her vulva was exposed. Holding onto headboard over his head, she started riding his tongue and lips. He lapped up her sweet pussy juice. It was wetter than he thought it had been.

"Suck on my clit," she ordered, breathless.

"Yes, mistress," he muttered around her pussy. He found her clit and started sucking.

Now she was bucking against his face, riding him. She was riding him harder and harder, her thighs squeezing against his ears. Her juice was dripping down his chin and cheeks. She tasted sweet and salty, tangy. Like perfect pussy.

"Harder," she moaned. He complied, unable to say his "yes, mistress" with his tongue and lips otherwise occupied.

She was bucking hard now. It was almost painful. He knew he couldn't stop his task. She moaned deeper, and started fucking his face, using the headboard as leverage as she rode against him.

Finally she gasped and arched her back, and he could tell she was cumming. He slid his tongue inside her and felt the throbbing as her whole body shuddered.

"Mmm, good boy," she moaned. She pulled herself off of his face and kissed him. "Good, good boy," she said. She was stroking his cock as she cooed in his ear. "That was very good. But I want to feel your cock in me when I do that again."

She leaned over the side of the bed away from him. He realized she was reaching into a bag. She pulled out two things and held them in her hands before him. One was a butt plug, he realized, and the other was a small vibrator.

"Hold this," she said, and handed him the butt plug. She reached back over the bed and got one more thing out of the bag. This time it was lube.

"Hold out your hand," she said.

"Yes, mistress," he said, and held his hand out to receive several squirts of lube.

"Rub that all over that plug," she told him.

"Yes, mistress." He followed her orders as she got on her hands and knees in front of him.

"Stick that in my ass," she ordered.

"Yes, mistress," he said, sitting up on his knees and doing as she said. He slid the silver cone with the jeweled handle on the end into her ass, gently. She moaned as he did so. It was a tight fit. She had turned on the vibrator and was using it on pussy as she leaned on her elbows.

"Rub the rest of the lube on your cock," she ordered.

"Yes, mistress." He did so, stroking himself and enjoying how hard he still was. His cock was throbbing and red.

"Now fuck me," she ordered. "Hard."

"Yes, mistress."

He entered her, slowly, feeling the sensation of her extremely tight pussy around his cock. The butt plug made her pussy feel much different than anything he'd ever been inside before. The texture was different. She was still sopping wet, but he was glad he had the lube, because she was so tight.

She gasped as he entered her. He could feel her vibrator on his shaft through her skin. She was rubbing it back and forth, forward and backward, and when he was fully inside of her, he could feel her holding it against his balls. It felt amazing. He started thrusting.

"Harder," she said.

"Yes, mistress."

He held onto her hips and thrust harder and faster.

"More,' she insisted.

"Yes, mistress," he gasped. This wasn't going to last long, he knew. He kept going, harder, faster, watching her ass ripple with every thrust.

"Spank me," she moaned.

"Yes, mistress," he said gratefully. He slapped her ass, one cheek and then the other.

"Harder," she said again.

"Yes, mistress." He slapped her ass again, harder. He knew he would leave handprints.

He kept thrusting, pulling her against him, deeper and deeper. He got lost in the sound of her vibrator, moving across her clit and his balls.

She was gasping every time he thrust into her, moaning, "Oh, yes, yes," making it so hard for him not to cum.

Almost as soon as he thought he couldn't handle it anymore, he felt her cum again, this time with her pussy wrapped around his cock. "Don't stop," she gasped, and he kept thrusting. "Mmm, yes," she hissed. He slapped her ass again while she throbbed around him. He could smell her pussy mixing with her vanilla perfume, her ass quivering against his stomach while his cock pounded her over and over.

"Are you going to cum for me?"

He moaned. "Yes, mistress," and kept thrusting.

Finally, he released. He shuddered and moaned and roped inside of her, over and over, the hardest orgasm he thought he'd ever had.

"Yes," she said, still holding the vibrator against her clit. She came again while he filled her with his cum. It was unbelievably hot.

Finally he pulled out and collapsed back on the bed. He heard the vibrator stop and a light thunk as it hit the ground. She turned around and collapsed against him, both of them catching their breaths.

"I'm so glad you didn't say pineapple," she laughed, kissing him on the cheek.

He laughed. "Yeah, me too," he said. They breathed hard, saying nothing for a few minutes.

"I think you'd better get dressed and go to your own room," she said.

He was relieved. "Yes, mistress," he said dutifully. He had to get up early for the flight and he slept terribly with someone else.

She got under the covers, still in the lace catsuit, and watched him get dressed. As he was putting on his shoes, she said, "We should do this again sometime."

He leaned back and kissed her full on the mouth. "Yes, mistress," he agreed.

He stood up to go, unsure whether or not she'd see him out. She looked ready to fall asleep. "You can turn off the light as you go," she waved, and rolled over, hugging a pillow and sighing happily.

"Yes, mistress," he agreed. He turned back as he opened the door and got one last look at her. Her eyes were closed and she may have already been asleep. He flipped off the lights and closed the door gently behind him.

Extreme Desire

The biggest problem with Andrei was that he couldn't keep his dick up. He was a smoker, which was a bad starting place. But he was also dealing with a lot -- dissolving a company with an ornery former partner, bankruptcy, starting a new business, debating applying for U.S. citizenship or going back home to Romania. When we met in the summer it was just supposed to be a freewheeling fun time. Sex was on the table from the second we met. We were both just oozing sex. He had nice hands -- one of my top criteria -- sexy arms, bald head, hot Romanian accent. We had several drinks for a first date and wandered back to my place for more, sitting on my back patio, chit chatting, kissing.

But then I was someone he could like too much -- naturally thoughtful, a good listener, conscientious, talented, funny, smart, on top of sexy, tall, fit, tan, smiling. A good cook. I had a cute dog, a good-paying job, my own home. Lots of friends. A robust social life, talents coming out of my ears. Good taste in music. A love of art and literature and everything that makes life worth living. A good whiskey collection.

So he couldn't just rail me and be done with it. He had to think about it. And thinking is the antithesis of sex. Especially for a man over 40 with a lot of other things on his mind.

"This hasn't been a problem before," he assured me as we took a break in my bed, cuddling, my pussy throbbing hungrily under the sheets.

I shrugged. It had been for me, in fact, since I was a teenager. The first guy I ever slept with couldn't keep it up the whole three times we tried when I was 17 and he was 20. He'd even asked me, sheepishly, if we could say we were still virgins because neither of us had ever had an orgasm. I'd told him sure, whatever.

And now that I was in my late 30s, it was more and more common. In fact, he was the third man this summer who'd had this issue. "Out of shape," was the first one's reasoning. Which he was. And stressed, of course. A workaholic. The second one admitted he couldn't get his ex out of his head. "She's in there," he'd told me as we'd settled onto my pillows, the same way I was doing now with Andrei.

I knew this was a temporary issue. It was something that could be overcome. Patience, understanding, second or third chances ... these were the necessary tools to overcome erectile dysfunction. I'd definitely had fulfilling sex with men who'd had the problem in the past.

But tonight I didn't want to be patient or understanding. I was visibly disappointed, even as I told him it was ok.

"It's not," he said, turning to lean over me. I could smell his cologne mixing with his sweat, which was intoxicating. The hair on his chest shone in little curls in the candlelight. I wanted to devour him. He looked at me with the same energy and kissed me on the mouth, then looked me over once more.

He slid his hand between my thighs and found my slit, soaking wet from desire. He thumbed my clit gently and I inhaled sharply.

"Oh," he said, and clicked his tongue. "Someone wants something."

I nodded, maybe too enthusiastically. He shifted his weight and kissed between my breasts, his right hand still gently caressing me. He trailed his kisses down to my belly button, then looked up at me with his huge brown eyes to catch my expression. Sheer desire from me, still, pulsing throughout my whole body.

"Just so you know," I breathed as his kisses moved to my thighs and towards where his hand was working. "That doesn't usually work for me."

"No?" he asked after licking my clit gently.

"No," I said, although I was groaning with pleasure.

"Hm," he said, burying his face between my thighs again as I squirmed. He slid a thick finger into my tight pussy while he licked the clit again, concentrating on being light and slow. I could tell he wanted to move faster, but he knew what he was doing. After a few more moments, he sat up and reached over to his bedside table for his phone.

My stomach sank. He was going to leave me hot and bothered now and go do something else, I thought. Because he couldn't get off, he was going to abandon ship.

"What kind of porn do you like?" he asked, his handsome face lighting up in the brightness of the screen as he scrolled.

"Huh?"

"You must watch porn," he said, looking up over the screen at me.

"Oh," I said. No one had ever asked me that before. Of course I watched porn. But could I admit what I liked to a man I had just met that night? "Multiple orgasms," I blurted without thinking.

"Really?" he said. He was typing it in.

"Multiple creampies," I corrected him.

He glanced back up and cocked an eyebrow. "Too messy for me," he said, "but if it works for the lady…" He handed the phone to me. "You pick." He returned to the wet between my legs while I scrolled slightly and settled on a video with a description along the lines of "five creampies, two cumshots", punctuated with all-caps descriptions of the youth or hotness of the girl involved and the size of the cock doing the cumming.

Andrei wasted no time getting back to work with his tongue while I moved the video through whatever storyline was at the beginning. He was sucking on my clit, still gentle, and I had to pause to adjust to the pleasure.

"Oh god yes!" came a woman's voice, overwhelmingly terrible in its fake enthusiasm. It was the phone. I started and turned the volume off, embarrassed.

"I hate the fake noises the women make," I explained. Andrei chuckled around my clit and nodded slightly, not taking his attention from my pleasure.

I settled back into watching the porn while Andrei kept working on me with his tongue, his lips, his whole mouth. I fast forwarded a little more to the first male orgasm -- a cum shot on the woman's stomach. I imagined the sound the man was making while he roped sticky wetness all over her, the gasping sounds while he let himself go. And then he slid his cock back into her and went right back to pounding her.

This was my absolute favorite idea, a man who couldn't get enough, who would just keep his dick hard and keep cumming over and over.

Andrei felt my excitement and put his thick finger back into my wetness. "God you're tight," he mumbled. I grabbed my free hand on the back of his head and bucked against him some, riding his face.

"I know," I responded, looking back to the porn. I fast forwarded a little more, this time to a point where the man flipped the woman over and was fucking her doggy style from behind. Again I watched with rapt attention as the man was clearly cumming, tensing up his thighs, inside her this time. He held his cock at the base and was pumping into her. Again I imagined the sounds he must have been making, the absolute pleasure he was succumbing to. And what the woman must have been feeling, knowing she was making him feel that way.

Andrei's finger was moving in and out of me now, faster and faster. He added a second finger, almost too much for me. He was using his whole mouth on my clit and my pussy. It was sloppy and noisy and wet.

As the man in the video pulled his cock out to show the creampie, he jerked himself off a little more, finishing on her ass a little bit. He was catching his breath silently for us, and then he pushed back in and just went right back to pounding the woman, who had a huge ass.

Suddenly I tensed up, gasping, and moaned louder than I'd moaned ever before, at least during sex. My pussy tensed up around Andrei's fingers and my thighs squeezed his head. He kept licking while I bucked against him.

"Mmmhmm," he breathed again with his incredibly sexy deep voice, enjoying my loss of control at his hands.

"Fuuuck," I gasped. I lay spreadeagle now, completely spent, the phone somewhere on the bed. Andrei watched me from between my legs, amused, resting his head in both hands.

"That doesn't work for you?" he asked, chuckling.

"No," I said. "Not usually." I closed my eyes and caught my breath. I pulled him up from his spot between my legs and kissed him, then pushed him back onto the pillows. I found his phone and picked it back up, opening the search bar on the porn site.

"Your turn," I said. "What's your favorite porn?"

He watched me for a moment, debating whether or not to answer truthfully. "Rope porn," he told me after a beat. I typed it in and handed him the results to scroll through.

"Whatever floats your boat," I told him, taking his soft cock in my right hand and slipping my mouth over the tip.

"Indeed," he said, watching me for another moment until he turned his attention to the phone screen

Just a Crush

I am pretty sure everyone in my office knew I had a crush on Carlos. I couldn't help it. He was gorgeous. Not too tall but tall enough (I'm not a size queen), dark skin, dark hair, green eyes, lightly muscled but not overbuilt. Like he did yard work in his spare time or ran on weekends, not like he spent all his time at the gym. Like he cared about what he ate but didn't turn down a slice of cake when it was someone's birthday.

He was funny, too. Anytime we chatted in the kitchen I'd linger a bit too long, joking with him about whatever TV show I was watching on Netflix or someone on the executive team saying something stupid. I'd try not to be obvious but I always hoped our hands would graze each other reaching for a coffee mug or getting something out of the fridge. It never happened.

Carlos was friendly to me but he wasn't interested. I knew he had a girlfriend. I wasn't even the person he hung out with at work the most – that was definitely Nikki. People joked about them being an item but it was clear they were just work spouses who spent their time together. They vibed well but it wasn't romantic. The energy was purely platonic. They grew up in the same neighborhood. I think Carlos was even friends with Nikki's husband.

Carlos and I both worked as customer service reps, but he was highly technical and I was just starting out, so we sat on opposite sides of the call center. Sometimes I'd hear him finish a call and I knew he was going to get up and head to the kitchen so I'd try to time my coffee or water runs accordingly, just to joke around at the sink or the fridge together. I'd try to take lunch at least five minutes after him, so it wasn't too obvious, but I'm sure my coworkers saw me lurking, gazing just a little too longingly as he walked past.

I had fantasies about running into him outside of work, at a bar or a neighborhood barbecue or something. We'd have friends in common somewhere. He'd have just gotten into a fight with his girlfriend, or she would have decided not to come out for some dumb reason, so he'd see me and we'd get to talking. We'd buy each other drinks. He'd admit he noticed me, saw me at the office, liked what I brought for lunch. Or that we both liked Diet Dr. Pepper. Or how I wore his favorite color (green) all the time.

And then we'd dance together, innocently at first, getting closer and closer... eventually in the dark of the club we'd start necking, he'd grab me, kiss me, call a cab, we'd be those two in the backseat tearing each other's clothes off...

Then we'd get back to my place and...

The thought of it sent shivers down my spine. I wanted him so badly. I wanted to run into him randomly anywhere I went. If I went to Target to get a new candle on the weekend, I'd hope he would be there. I'd hope to see him at a bus stop near our work. I'd hope he came to happy hour with the CR team on a Friday afternoon (he never did, and I always left early because of it). I'd will him to appear, even with his girlfriend, at a movie theater or a stroll through the park. I just wanted to see him.

But our paths never crossed. We lived very different lives. He'd never go to the clubs I went to, and I'd never go anywhere he went. Except work.

I looked at his public Instagram account without following him. I never looked at his stories because I didn't want him to know that I was watching. He posted enough for me to see that he had a good family life, spent time with his mom and sisters, took his girlfriend to dinner and the club on weekends (ugh). They didn't live together but they might as well. They went to the gym together (which somehow didn't interrupt my fantasy that he was just naturally built the way he was), they went to car shows together, they went on family vacations together. She knew his mom, too.

I stalked his girlfriend, of course. Not in a scary way. I just looked at her public posts, too, or the ones he tagged her in. She was pretty. Maybe a little plain. Nothing like the glowing, gorgeous, funny man he was. At least not like the one he was in my crush-addled brain.

I thought about asking him for a ride home. He had a real muscle car, a Dodge Charger, it was bright orange and loud, and it was his pride and joy. I rode the bus to and from work on a tight schedule, because it only came every 20 minutes, and if you missed it, you had to wait around, maybe longer after work with traffic. I wished that I'd miss the bus home once, and he'd see me standing at the bus stop, waiting, and offer me a ride. Or maybe my manager would ask me to stay late and get overtime because someone had called out sick, and me and Carlos would be the only two people left at the end of the night because he'd be working late, too, and he'd offer me a ride because he didn't want me waiting at the bus stop alone after dark.

"Come on," he'd say, bypassing all my shy hesitation. "It's late, it won't be that far out of the way."

He'd rev the engine and show off how fast he could drive. I love fast cars, I'd tell him. He'd go even faster. He'd put his hand on my knee when he put the car in sixth gear, speeding through the night. We'd give each other meaningful glances, he'd keep his hand on my knee except when he was changing gears, the whole ride. When he got to my apartment, he'd park, without asking, and follow me up the front stoop. We'd be kissing before I got the front door open. By the third floor, we'd both have our shirts off, our pants unzipped…

But our time together was limited to the times I could successfully time my breaks to his at work, maybe a moment or two in the morning or evenings when we were packing up, a hello on our ways to or from the bathroom or a team meeting. If he knew who I was beyond my first name, he didn't let on. I never got an accidental "like" or view of one of my stories on Instagram from him. He never bought me a Diet Dr. Pepper from the vending machine and put it on my desk and asked if I wanted to go on a walk around the building for this break. And he certainly never asked me if I needed a ride home.

I had my own work spouse, Clarice. She was probably 30 years older than me and was the main receptionist. She and I went on walks together, me with a Diet Dr. Pepper and she with a plain seltzer ("I can't do the caffeine after lunch," she'd whine, "I'm over 50, I'd never sleep again"), talking shit about our coworkers and our home lives. She had a husband. I had a cat. I don't know how we decided to bond to each other, but we did. Just one of those things.

She knew I had a crush on Carlos but definitely not the extent to which it affected my full day. I usually took lunch and my two 15-minute breaks with her, and sometimes she'd laugh when I was late. "Carlos kept you again, hm?" She didn't know how I longed to touch him, hear his voice, just look at him.

Except maybe she did. Because one day as we were walking she brought up the most random thing.

"Oh my god, you won't believe this," she said, lowering the loudness of her normal chit chat to the level she usually reserved for extra juicy gossip, like knowing someone was about to be terminated or the head of accounting had sexually harassed another intern and it was being swept under the rug again.

"What?" I asked, similarly low, looking around to make sure no one could hear us on the sidewalk as we walked around the building.

"So you know I'm in this women's book club group," Clarice went on. I did. She talked about it almost as much as she did her dumb husband. "Well one of the girls has started selling… get this… sex toys."

"Ha," I laughed. For me, it wasn't a big deal. Everyone had sex toys. So many of my friends had tried selling them as part of a multi-level marketing scheme that they had boxes of leftovers, lube, vibrators, anal plugs, just sitting in their closets. But for a woman over 50, I'm sure it was very exciting. "Did you buy anything?"

"Oh, god, no," Clarice said. Too bad, I thought, her husband would probably be thrilled. "But it got us all to talking about porn."

Oh boy, I thought. Old lady porn. Gross. But it was Clarice, so it would at least be funny.

"Like OnlyFans?" I asked. Was one of her friends trying to make it big on OnlyFans? Oh, how gross that would be. Maybe a foot fetish theme? That wouldn't be so bad. I guessed people liked grannies sometimes. I shook my head at the thought. Not for me. Fit, hot, men. That's what I liked to see.

"Maybe," she said, clearly trying to remember. "I don't know, it was something online. It wasn't for sale or anything, it was free. But one of the girls was saying this guy was demonstrating how to use the sex toys and he was really good at it so she wanted to show us."

That was much better than what I was expecting. Tamer, probably, too. I'm not sure what kind of kink I had thought Clarice would get into with her girls but this was probably the best outcome for my own internal imagination.

What she said next floored me.

"But the thing is, the guy who does it –" and here she leaned in conspiratorially and stopped walking, so we both had to pause "-- well you know that guy Carlos in tech support? The one you think is cute?"

"Yeah," I said. My heart stopped at the mention of his name. "What about him?" Did I know Carlos in tech support? What was she kidding?

"Well that's who this guy looked like!" Clarice clapped her hands together, laughing.

"No way," I said, trying to sound floored by the joke of it, rather than the possibility that maybe, somewhere, I could watch Carlos playing with sex toys, for free.

"Totally," she said. "Not exactly, but, you know, similar. He's a cute one, that Carlos." We resumed our walking.

"Yeah," I said. I thought for a moment of the possibilities. What if it was him? What if it was Carlos? "Are you sure it wasn't him? I know some people do that kind of stuff for side gigs these days." My heart pounded, my throat was dry, my palms were sweaty.

"I don't think so," she said, unsure of herself. "I think the guy's name was Don something. Don Rockhard, something silly like that."

"Right," I said. We took another few steps, she drank her flavored fizzy water. My Diet Dr. Pepper got warm. "He could be using a pseudonym."

"Oh, I don't think so," she laughed it off. I realized I was pressing the issue too much. "He doesn't seem like that kind of guy. But I thought you might think it was funny. I know you think he's cute, too."

She made it sound like my all-consuming crush was the same as everyone else's in the office. We all just thought Carlos was cute. And that was it.

"I do," I said, laughing with her. And then we did another lap and finished our sodas and changed the subject so many times I don't even know what else we talked about.

I had trouble concentrating on my work all afternoon. Not that anything I did was too strenuous, but I wasn't going to hit my big targets in any real way. I was ahead for the week, anyway, so it didn't matter, but I hoped no one would notice. I was so absorbed in my own thoughts that I hardly noticed when Carlos left work a few minutes early, turning off his monitor and waving to the other guys in tech support. His replacement had gotten in early. I barely looked up from my own monitor to watch him get in his car out the window next to me, a ritual I looked forward to every day.

The bus ride home was excruciating. I knew I couldn't Google this guy while I was on the bus, some creeper would see over my shoulder and say something. But Don Rockhard, the guy demonstrating sex toys for a bunch of 50-year-old women, could he be Carlos? My Carlos?

When I got up the stairs to my third floor walkup, I barely greeted my cat appropriately. She was very confused, and tried to brush up against my legs, but I was on a mission. I rushed past her meows to my bedroom where my laptop was on my bed from my morning Facetime with my sister. I decided this exploration needed the full screen, not just my dinky phone.

I opened up a browser in "incognito mode" and typed in the guy's name.

"Don Rockhard"

I thought for a minute and added "sex toys" for good measure. I didn't want the wrong Don Rockhard.

"Did you mean 'dom rockhard sex toys'?" Google came back, with a slew of results for just that.

Of course it was "Dom".

I clicked on the first video, breathlessly, not noticing the description, just a thumbnail with a dark guy in miniature.

And there in all his glory was a Carlos lookalike, naked from the waist up with oiled, huge muscles (not like Carlos) and tight light wash jeans (also something Carlos would never wear). He was kissing a woman in lingerie (boring) and eventually he pushed her onto the bed. He pulled out a Hitachi wand and started using it on her, making her scream multiple times (ridiculous) before he unbuttoned his pants to let an enormous hard cock pop out of it.

I paused and just looked at this. I was so turned on. The thought of Carlos having a hard on was almost too much for me. I felt down my own pants and started touching myself.

The next video was even better, with Carlos and another man using a metal wand on each other. There weren't the phony screams like there were with the women, and there was a lot of rubbing lube on each other's huge pecs and arms and butts and thighs. There were a lot of angles. And they both came like volcanoes, one right after the other, helplessly gushing, sweating, gasping.

I did the same, and found another video to watch. And another. Even after I was utterly spent I got my fill of my new Carlos, just as unattainable as the real one, but performing for me in a fantasy that the real Carlos never would.

I fell asleep in the light of the computer screen, without eating dinner or anything. I woke up at 4 in the morning, sticky with myself and with the cat meowing angrily for her dinner. I stumbled up and fed her, washed my face and hands and whatever else needed a rinse, and got back into bed, where I fell asleep again to more Dom Rockhard and his coterie of toys and partners succumbing to their charms.

I woke up early, starving, but satisfied. I pleasured myself to a quick video of Dom again – a repeat from the night before – and headed to the shower, clear headed and happy. I almost felt like whistling. I felt better than I had in months.

I got to the office early, made myself coffee, and logged in to start taking calls. My boss sauntered in a few minutes after me and gave me a thumbs up. "No overtime, though," she said as she closed her office door. I shrugged. I'd log out early if I had to. At least she'd noticed I was early to work, a real team player, I'm sure she'd say. I'd even beat Clarice to the office.

I didn't even notice Carlos pulling up in his Charger, or watch him pour himself coffee, or fix a new pot (he was so thoughtful). I was honestly texting a friend when he sat down at his monitor, and I had already left for my walk with Clarice before he took his first break. I didn't even talk to him at all the entire day.

Had Dom broken Carlos's spell?

That night I went home and was a little less obsessed with my new favorite porn star, but I was looking forward to another evening in. I fed my cat on time and made myself dinner, at least. I even managed to call my mother and talk for half an hour before Dom Rockhard pulled me into his orbit. But dissatisfied with the videos available to me on the free site, I decided to find out more about him.

There was a Dom Rockhard fan club, apparently, full of people who, like me, were obsessed with how good he was. Men, women, non-binary, gender neutral, it didn't matter; he hit a nerve among all kinds of fans. We all loved his body, his voice, his stroke, how he used his hands, how he used the toys, the noises he made, how he looked when he came.

"My girl caught me watching him and saw how much I searched for him in my search history," one straight guy said on a podcast about him. "And I told her I was watching the guy to be a better lover for her."

"What'd she say to that?" laughed his co-host.

"Oh, she was still so mad," he said, "until I had her watch one of the videos. And now she doesn't want anything to do with me. Just him."

Why had I never learned of this glorious man before? Was it because he mostly did straight porn and I didn't watch much of that? He had a gay following, too, and he was apparently friendly to any of his fans, no matter how they identified. Even lesbians loved him. He had just been magically hidden from me.

My days at work got easier. My crush on Carlos disappeared. Compared to my angel Dom, he was boring – too straight, too slim, too normal. Dom was a lover and he had a gift. Carlos was just another guy with a girlfriend who went to the same clubs on the weekend and cared about his car more than anything else.

Clarice noticed. "You're glowing," she told me. "Have you met someone?"

"Nope," I told her, shrugging. "Just enjoying my alone time more than usual."

I was still going out with my friends and shopping at Target, of course. I just wasn't spending so much energy wishing Carlos would magically appear there, too.

And then one day, an ad popped up in my Instagram stories that hit me like an arrow through the heart.

"Meet internet sensation Dom Rockhard," a voice boomed in my headphones. I was at work on a break. Clarice was at the doctor and I was alone in the breakroom drinking my Diet Dr. Pepper. "Live and in person at the Adult Entertainment Expo." I put the phone face down on the table and looked around. Had anyone seen it? No one else was anywhere nearby. I quickly closed Instagram and went back to my desk.

The fact that I was getting ads for this meant that I wasn't being careful enough in my browsing, I realized, but of course I wasn't. I was a proud member of the Dom Rockhard fan club, contributing to Reddit threads about him, following him on Instagram, liking his stories, reading fan fiction about him... I was committed. And now was my chance to meet him in person.

I waited until I was home that night to find out more details about the expo. It was a month away at a big convention center downtown. I could get there on the bus. Tickets were pricey, but to see Dom, to get to meet Dom, would be entirely worth it. I'd just have to skip a happy hour or two, order takeout one night less.

I'd go alone, I realized. None of my friends knew about my obsession with this porn star, just as I hadn't ever discussed my obsession with Carlos. But this felt less obsessive and more... enjoyable. It wasn't agonizing. I didn't wish Dom would just show up on my Target run. I knew he never would. I got to enjoy his sexuality without wishing I could see him in person. It was a much more freeing feeling than a crush on a real person in my real life.

Which was why it was so surprising when, three days before the Saturday I was slated to meet Dom Rockhard with thousands (or at least hundreds? I had no idea) of other adoring fans at the Adult

Entertainment Expo, I ran into him at the Target by myself.

We were both in line for Starbucks. It was late and they were closing but I had decided I deserved a treat before I trudged the long blocks home. I had popped into Target to get more face moisturizer because I was completely out. There was a broad-shouldered man in front of me, wearing a tight shirt and a plain black baseball cap. He was taller than me, but not too much. And he was confused.

"I just have no idea what I want to get," he shrugged to me and the very annoyed barista. "Maybe you go ahead of me."

I knew the voice. I knew the face.

"Sure," I said, staring at him, but trying not to be too obvious. "I'll have a venti mango dragon fruit lemonade Refresher."

The barista nodded and wrote my order on the cup, then rang me up.

"That sounds amazing," Dom said. "I'll have the same. Put 'em both on my tab."

I was absolutely agog as he pulled out a Starbucks card and paid for both drinks. The barista did not care one lick. She was just glad to have us both out of her hair.

"Wow," I said. "Thank you so much."

"Thank you for making up my mind," he said. He offered his hand. "Dom," he said.

"This is going to be weird," I said, taking his hand. "But I know. I'm a huge fan."

He grinned bashfully like a little schoolgirl. "You are?"

"Oh my gosh, yes," I gushed. I could feel myself blushing. "I'm in your fan club, really."

"I can't believe it," he said. "I've never run into a fan before."

I had just touched him. I was talking to him. And the world was still spinning. Everything was in order. I hadn't said anything stupid. I hadn't embarrassed myself. It was all natural and easy.

And would you believe we talked the entire night? We sat at the Starbucks sipping our fruity lemonades until the barista shut all the lights off on us, and then strolled the aisles of Target giggling at the seasonal things for sale for a dollar and the weird decor of the month, smelling all the candles, and picking out the best nail polish colors until they, too, kicked us out. And then he asked me if he could buy me a drink.

There was one bar in the strip mall, and we closed it down, too, him with a straight whisky and me with a frozen margarita. We kept finding things to talk about.

When they finally kicked us out of the restaurant at midnight, he asked if he could drive me home. And I accepted.

He had a Ford Mustang, all souped up and clean and even nicer (and faster) than Carlos's. He opened the door for me on the passenger side and closed it gently once I was situated.

"I love fast cars," I told him as he revved the engine. He grinned and peeled out of the parking lot, me screaming with glee.

When he got the car in gear, he put his hand on my knee. We shot each other knowing glances.

At my apartment, he parked, and without saying a word, got out of the car and opened my door, helping me out. He didn't let go of my hand. He walked me up the steps of my front stoop and we stood facing each other.

"So," he said.

"So," I said. My heart was pounding, but manageably. It was a pleasant pounding, not a doomed pounding. I was enjoying this.

He was bashful and brought a hand up behind his head, looking around.

"This was fun," he said.

"It was," I answered.

Another beat.

"Look," he said, "you know what I do for a living."

"I think it's wonderful," I said.

"I love that," he smiled. "But it's just, when I really like someone, I like to take it slow."

"And you really like me?"

Who was I, with these cool, calm lines?

"I do," he nodded, grinning from ear to ear.

"Well, I like you, too."

He leaned in and kissed me on the cheek, almost chaste.

"Can I ask for your number?" he said.

"Of course," I smiled.

We kissed after we exchanged numbers, a passionate kiss, but just a promise of things to come. He watched me get into my apartment building safely, and then danced his way to the car.

I got VIP access at his event, and he made sure my ticket was comped. He lived nearby in the city, it ended up, and while he traveled some for conferences, we saw each other every weekend. It wasn't long before he was my boyfriend.

But it never went past kissing in those first few months. He really meant what he'd said about going slow. I even came to watch him on set a few times, and while it was hot, we never went any further until it was really right for both of us. (Although I did get a lot of use out of the free toys he got to try, on my own time.)

It's been years. We live together, and in fact, we're planning our wedding. Yes, we've sealed the deal, and no, I won't give you the sordid details. You'll just have to imagine, or maybe look up some of his work and pretend you're me.

May September

Marcella couldn't help it -- she was bored. The man across from her couldn't even be saved by the expensive Chardonnay he'd ordered for the table. He was dull. He talked only about money and investing, and never asked Marcella a question about herself. She was polite enough to let him drone on, but she knew she would be paying for this dinner, and he would be leaving alone, even if he didn't know it.

The food was good, at least -- a lovely poached salmon, such a ladylike thing for a woman of 45 to order. Healthy enough to offset the two gin martinis she'd had waiting for her date to arrive. He had been late, of course, because he was already in a relationship with his work. He thought this was a positive about him -- "I'm a workaholic," he'd said with a smile, as if it was something to strive toward. In Marcella's mind, it meant he had discovered a way to never have to work on any of his personal relationships, or even a way to have affairs so he could keep everything as shallow as he possibly could. Her first two husbands had been "workaholics". So had she.

She found it unbearable now. And she despised men who thought it was a positive personality trait.

He had only gotten more boring from there. Ordering the most expensive bottle of wine on the menu, even though it didn't go at all with his dinner (the most expensive steak, which he'd ordered well done, somehow). He was rude to the servers. He was demanding and entitled. She half expected him to bellow, "Do you know who I am?" at the poor sommelier. His clothes, while tailored, were generic. His shoes were scuffed, she'd noted. His fingernails were an absolute mess, which meant he would be a terrible lover. The only question he'd asked her had been about her work, specifically, her former work, because that was the thread by which they'd been introduced.

"Yes," she'd told him, "I used to work with Stan at Merrill."

"I love Stan!" this date had exclaimed. "He's a real asset to the team now. So glad he thought to introduce us. What a guy, huh." He'd winked a little and put a forkful of steak into his mouth.

Indeed, she'd thought. She was sure Stan was laughing about this. She owed him from the horrible date she'd set him up with last month -- a part-time nurse, part-time go-go dancer she'd known through friends who had abs for days and, she thought, could have spiced up Stan's boring routine of preppy boys in MBA programs. Stan had tried a single date with this interesting, almost age-appropriate change of pace, but they'd had nothing in common and still gone home together and it had been a disaster, and Stan had been seething in humorous silence ever since.

And now Marcella saw how he'd exacted his revenge: This fellow. Was it Doug? Donald? She'd forgotten before the date had even started, and now he was sitting across from her, boring her to tears.

He didn't ask her why she'd left finance, or to tell him about her current work, which she thought was far more interesting. He even went on a long talking spree about how important crypto was and the terrors of the unwashed masses (he didn't literally call them "unwashed masses", but that was the impression he gave) investing in things like Game Stop or AMC without guidance.

He was still droning on. He was probably going to order dessert.

Marcella swirled her wine and pretended to listen, politely. She was being pretty obviously disinterested. He was so boring he couldn't pick up on her cues. She was sure he would throw an absolute hissy fit when she refused to go home with him. Which was why she was going to insist on paying, at least for her half. And she was almost looking forward to his man tantrum as a palate cleanser, at least an interesting end to a terrible date.

What was most interesting about this man was what was going on over his shoulder. Behind him, Marcella could see a very, very young woman who was having dinner with a much older man. This restaurant had a reputation for being very romantic and very expensive. If this was a date, it was an impressive date for the woman, or was meant to be. This was the kind of place that wealthy people went to show off (like Marcella's date). The young woman was certainly the youngest person in the room, younger even than all the servers. The man she was with was more reasonably aged for the circumstances -- at least in his 50s. Was he her father? Her sugar daddy? Her uncle? A legitimate date? A professor?

"Where are your investments?" Marcella's date asked, startling her out of her reverie. "Mostly equities, right?"

"Real estate," Marcella said, lying. She owned the apartment she lived in here and a condo on a beach and that was it. Not enough to be considered "invested" in real estate. She sipped her wine.

"Oof, that's not a bad answer," her date said, "but really, I think crypto is the way to go." And he kept babbling.

Marcella took another sip of the lovely Chardonnay -- she tried not to gulp it -- and looked back at the couple over her date's shoulder. The young woman looked as bored as Marcella was. The man had his back to her, and Marcella could just see how gray his hair was. He had broad shoulders and looked substantial and fit. He was probably handsome, for his age. Was he talking that woman's ear off as badly as Marcella's date was talking hers?

She examined the food on the table. A perfectly reasonable bottle of Cabernet Sauvignon to go with his steak (of course, that's what men ordered at this restaurant, but at least it appeared to be medium rare) and the young woman was having red meat, too. How charming was that, Marcella thought. Most of the young women she encountered these days were vegan, or at least didn't eat red meat -- a thinly veiled way to be anorexic and passively morally righteous at the same time.

The woman wasn't drinking her wine, though, which Marcella thought was a shame. She knew that bottle, and had seen it on the menu, and was disappointed when her date had opted for a more expensive white. But maybe the woman was afraid of being drunk with this man.

Marcella felt the need to help her. Or at least to figure out what was going on. The woman was gorgeous -- dark olive skin, green eyes, jet black hair ironed stock straight in shining curtains around her brooding face.

Another sip of wine and Marcella said, "Will you excuse me?" mid-sentence for Don or Doug or Dan, and stood up, grabbing her handbag and putting her napkin in her chair. A server was behind her immediately to scoot the chair out for her, fold the napkin, make sure everything was silently right as it should be.

The date had no time to ask what she was doing, and she made for the ladies' room, although when she was out of sight of the man at her table, Marcella went to the maître d', Stephen, and pulled him aside.

"I need to send a note to the woman at table 10," she said, gesturing slightly with her hand. What her date hadn't known was that Marcella came to this restaurant all the time. She practically lived at the bar. She'd slept with at least two former servers. She tipped well and never got too drunk to be embarrassing. The staff adored her. And she knew the place like the back of her hand, including its regulars.

"Of course, madam," Stephen said. He quickly produced a pen and piece of paper, as well as a neat notepad on which she could write.

Marcella scribbled quickly, handed the note to Stephen, and said, "Now would be good."

"Certainly, madam," he said, charmed by the intrigue, and briskly headed to the young woman to hand her the folded note.

Marcella watched it be delivered from around the corner discreetly, watched the woman read it, watched her brighten at the excuse to get up from her place. As the young woman excused herself, Marcella made haste to the ladies' room, where she busied herself in front of one of the big bright mirrors, reapplying her light pink lipstick.

The young woman practically burst through the door and glanced around.

"Christ," she said in her London lilt, "I thought you'd never come for me."

She practically attacked the older woman, kissing her passionately, pushing her into the mirror, smudging both their lipsticks, her dark purple with Marcella's champagne pink. Marcella burst out laughing.

"It was just so fun to watch you be so bored," she said between kisses. "Was he as awful as I thought he'd be?"

"Absolutely dreadful," the young woman said, leaving purple kiss marks up and down Marcella's neck now. The older woman was still laughing, enjoying the caresses, but keeping the younger woman at arm's length.

"Just don't get any lipstick on this dress," she laughed. "My date will suspect."

"Please, let him suspect," the young woman said, and took Marcella's face in her hands to deliver a full kiss on the mouth. Her hand crept up Marcella's dress, tight as it was, knowingly moving past the garter belt where Marcella's pussy lay bare, even while she had stockings on her legs.

Marcella sighed with the knowing, wishing they could give up the rest of the game and just spend the night here, fucking each other with their hands, while their dates waited and got restless and finally left. But these were older men. They were relentless. They'd send someone to check on them.

"I just had to check on you," Marcella said. "You really are being so obvious." She pushed the younger woman's hand away, pulled it out from her skirt and kissed it on the knuckles. "Soon, my angel. This will be so much better if we can finish the tease."

"You are truly terrible," the young woman laughed, and kissed Marcella's hand as well. She took a big inhale of her fingers, her eyes closed, before opening them, looking up meaningfully under long lashes at Marcella's face. "But you're right, this will enhance our later activities, I'm sure."

She turned to the mirror behind them, pulling a few tissues out from the box on a nearby shelf and wiping up what she could of their smudged lipsticks before pulling out the purple tube to reapply.

"I love that you don't wear that smudge proof nonsense," Marcella said, coming up behind her and putting her arms around her.

The young woman smiled; her teeth almost unbelievably white under the dark berry of the lipstick. She blotted on a tissue and blew a kiss at Marcella. "I know you do."

She turned around and held Marcella back, both beholding the other, taking in their scents. The young woman favored citrus, bergamot, and musk. Marcella wore florals, rose and gardenia and jasmine. Together they made quite a garden.

"Just drink a little of the wine at least," Marcella said. "It's such a good bottle."

The young woman scrunched up her face. "You know I don't drink much," she said.

"Yes, I know," Marcella agreed, letting her go. "At least bring it to the bar when you come, I'll drink it."

"It's a deal," the young woman said. She pecked Marcella on the cheek again and headed for the door.
"Oh, how's yours?" she asked with her hand on the doorknob.

"To use your word, dreadful," Marcella said, turning to the mirror to wipe the purple lipstick off her neck and face.

The young woman laughed and exited, leaving Marcella to her ablutions. She used the toilet, too, wiping up some of the wet from her pussy where the young woman had brought it to life.

"Well, that took forever," Marcella's date said tactlessly as she came back to the table, a server moving her chair effortlessly while she sat down, placing the napkin silently back in her lap. "I took the liberty of ordering you a scotch."

He motioned toward a horrible, expensive bit of smoke with a giant round rock in it. The server had certainly made a face when he ordered it and was probably trying to hide a face behind her now. Marcella hated smoky scotch and everyone in the place knew it. She could feel the bartender watching her, a knowing smile on his face that he couldn't hide.

"You know I think I'm quite done," Marcella said, raising a hand. A server appeared out of nowhere with the check, gleefully watching her produce a credit card from her purse and hand it to him without even looking at the bill.

"You're what?" said the man, his face growing red. "Hey, now, I was thinking we could get dessert—"

"I'm done," Marcella said. The young woman was trying not to watch from the table just in front of her, although she was facing Marcella and there was a laugh about to come bursting from her lips. The young woman took a sip of wine to compose herself, then turned to her date, all ears still on Marcella.

"Well I'm going to at least drink my scotch," the date said.

"You're welcome to," Marcella said. "You can have mine, too," and pushed the offending glass to him.

"It's the most expensive dram they have," he stammered, the color reaching his ears.

"I'm sure," Marcella said. She stood up, taking what was left of her Chardonnay as a server deftly pulled her chair back for her, and headed to the bar. "Good night."

The date was absolutely bewildered. The young woman was close to spitting out the sip of water she'd just taken. Marcella knew the woman would want to do the same to her date, but that wasn't part of the script. It was too early yet. She signed the bill at the bar and sat, watching the young woman and the rest of the room, striking up a conversation with Maria the bartender, pointedly ignoring Doug or Dan or Dave, whose back was to her now.

This was the trick of the evening, truly. Would he swallow his pride and get up and come to the bar and ask Marcella what had just happened? Would he take as long as he could savoring the drink? Would he swallow it in one go, or just abandon it and leave, knowing he'd been bested, for what reason or how he would never know? Would he try to find a younger woman to hit on in the place? All of these had been played out before with similar men, over long years of her coming to this restaurant, each boring man after the other suggesting it because it was expensive, not because he knew it was her favorite.

If they'd only asked, she thought, they would have known they were meeting her on her own turf.

This date sat sullenly, stunned, maybe a little stupid. He sipped his scotch, not looking at Marcella, not looking at anyone, not the server who asked him if he'd like something else. Not even his phone.

Marcella almost felt a little bad. But he was boring. And this was her game.

And then the real fireworks began.

The young woman – whose name was Zabeen, but Marcella always called her Zabi – stood up, offended, glaring at her much older date. A server arrived to move her chair but not quickly enough.

"No," she said, loudly. "Absolutely not. I don't care if you've paid for dinner."

Even watching him from behind, the man was flabbergasted. "What did I do?" Marcella heard him say.

Marcella's own date – drunk now, dejected – watched with great interest.

Zabi grabbed her wine. "I refuse."

She strutted up to the bar and took a seat.

"Refuse what?" the older man called after her. "I haven't suggest anything but dessert!"

Marcella's date watched the young woman sit at the bar with her wine, three seats away from Marcella.

"Women," he muttered, then raised his second scotch to the other date. "Am I right?" he said, more loudly.

The other man shook his head. He threw his napkin on the table and bolted, mortified and angry to be accused of something, even if he hadn't been accused outright. This was a nice restaurant, he was surely muttering to himself. The women – especially the young women – should be appreciative.

Zabi caught Maria's eye, pointed to the full glass of wine before her with just a smudge of purple berry lipstick on the rim, and pointed to Marcella.

"Rough night?" Maria said to Zabi with a twinkle in her eye. She gave the young woman a glass of ice water and scooted the glass of red wine over to Marcella knowingly. Zabi drank the water fully.

"Not yet," she winked, and looked at Marcella.

But the game wasn't over yet. Marcella resented their skipping a step. Zabi wasn't supposed to send the wine over yet, until they'd really started a conversation. But she'd finished her Chardonnay and was ready for this Cab, especially since it had been breathing for a while. It was one of her absolute favorites.

Her date was too soused and self righteous to notice, anyway, which would have been part of the fun. He kept on his scotch, one sip after another, sullenly scanning the room, maybe looking for a graceful exit. It made Marcella proud to know she'd probably ruined his night and he had no idea why.

Maria knew the game, and as she dropped the glass of wine in front of Marcella, announced, maybe a bit too loudly, "From the young lady in the velvet dress."

"Thank you," Marcella said, not missing a beat. She raised the glass to Zabi and took a sip. Zabi tipped an imaginary hat her way and took a sip of her water.

They all sat for a beat, Marcella's date muttering to himself, Maria polishing a glass, the din of the restaurant continuing carelessly around them. Marcella was the only regular tonight, which wasn't too unusual. Most everyone had a single night of the week they came, while she could be found here almost every night of the week. Zabi joined her when she could, although Zabi's job was very demanding. But whenever Marcella or Zabi had a dreadful date to go on, they'd ask the other to find one of her own so they could play this game. Which wasn't that often, all things considered. Maybe three times a year, depending on how angry Stan was with Marcella or who Zabi could find on Tinder.

"So what's your name?" Zabi asked in her charming London accent, leaning into Marcella, loud enough for the date to hear.

"Marcella," came the response. "But if you're going to hit on me, I'm too old for you anyway."

The "cut to the chase" script, they both knew. Zabi didn't miss a beat.

"How do you know that?" she asked.

"Who's better, Madonna or Britney?" Marcella asked.

"Who's what?" Zabi answered. This was a new question, but they both knew Zabi knew the right answer. It was always Madonna, for Marcella, anyway. Zabi had her own ideas when they were alone together in bed on Sunday mornings, Zabi showing Marcella a new TikTok trend. But Madonna was Marcella's favorite, Material Girl or Ray of Light, she didn't care.

"Too young," Marcella said, taking another sip of her wine.

"Why would I hit on you, anyway?" Zabi asked.

"Why wouldn't you?" Marcella countered.

The date's ears were perking up. Were these women hitting on each other? Had he turned his date gay? He peeked over the side of his booth at the bar, trying to be discreet but missing by a mile.

Zabi stood up at this point, bringing her glass of water with her to the seat next to Marcella.

"That's an excellent question," she answered. "So tell me your name then."

"Marcella," said the older woman.

Zabi held out her hand. "Zabi," she said.

They shook. And as they shook on it, Zabi pulled Marcella in for an unscripted kiss.

"And I'm taking you home with me tonight," she said after.

The date was shocked, clearly, but Maria hooted and clapped.

"Amazing," she said, without thinking. "So good."

Marcella shot her a glance, and Maria recollected herself. She went back to drying glasses and polishing them. Zabi was grinning ear to ear.

"You are trouble," Marcella said, as Zabi sat next to her. "Please, bartender, get this girl whatever she wants."

"I'll buy," Zabi said. "You look like a gin martini girl," she said to Marcella.

"Never after dinner," Marcella said, not missing a beat, still sipping her favorite wine. She loved Zabi's quickness and wit.

"Ah, then, a digestif for the lady," she called to Maria. "Amaro. Grappa."

"Maybe I like it sweet," Marcella said.

"Chartreuse, then," Zabi said. "Yellow if you have it."

"Too sweet," Marcella said. They smiled at each other.

Maria put a snifter each of green and yellow Chartreuse before them. They all knew Zabi preferred the sweeter yellow and Marcelle the more bitter green. "Cheers," she said.

Marcella finished her wine. She was tipsy enough now, with Zabi next to her, smelling her citrus perfume and youth. The date had finished his drink and got up in a huff. Too bad, he was going to miss the best part, she thought. The part where they fell in love.

They never could finish the script, not really. It was too hard to pretend. They knew each other too intimately. Maria joked that there was a couch in the ladies' room for the two of them to get each other off during the interlude Marcella always took, having Stephen deliver the note. But Marcella never let it get that far. It was all just a temptation to bring them home to each other.

But tonight Zabi was next to her, sliding her hand up her dress just a little at a time. Sober as a Baptist preacher with his deacons, Marcella knew – Zabi never drank more than a sip or two of wine. Marcella would have to finish her yellow Chartreuse, too.

She let Zabi's fingers wander a bit, touching the soft warmth of her thighs. She loved this game. They'd lean on each other for the quick walk home, and then finally, hungrily, they'd fall into each other and spend the entire night in ecstasy.

But just a minute more of the tease, Marcella hoped. To keep herself feeling as young as Zabi was. She kissed the younger woman on the mouth, to a hoot from Maria, before returning to her digestif.

Milestone Birthday

It was late, and they were drunk. Both of them, just hammered. That was the point of the evening, though. They'd been out on a run with their irreverent running group, both of them in dresses. His was a green long-sleeved number with shiny disco ball beading all over it, scandalously short above his knees. Hers was a long orange psychedelic maxi dress with basically no back, all straps, a little too big for her but hugging her ample ass. It was see-through, too; in the sunlight you could see her nipples and the fact that she wasn't wearing a shred of underwear. But it was hot. Underwear would've been another layer encumbering her skin from finding relief from the air.

They'd been drinking beer since 6:30. It was her 40th birthday and she'd led the run, forcing the group of 30 sweaty runners into bars in their dresses and make-up and tiaras. It was The Queen's Run for her birthday, and everyone was supposed to dress as a queen – preferably a drag queen. She bought everyone shots and pitchers of beer at the beer stops as they sweated through the humidity. And at the end of the night they made her drink a bottle of prosecco.

And now they were at the after party, on a patio at a bar where everyone else was somewhere between 22 and 29. There was karaoke. She loved karaoke. He loved to watch her sing karaoke. She made her way through a Whitney Houston song and then stumbled back out to the patio with him. Someone handed her another drink, and him. And they were both so drunk.

But she couldn't keep her hands off of him. She sat on his left side and her right hand crept up his dress, like she was a drunk frat boy getting handsy with a girl who was also just as drunk. She held onto his slim thigh like it was the only thing anchoring her to the patio, which it probably was. They made out, smiling at each other before biting into each other's lips, making the prudish younger people a little uncomfortable but not caring at all. It was delicious and free and they felt young and enjoyed each other's salty bodies, lips, hands, thighs. He held her close when they weren't kissing. They drank more.

Friends stopped by and talked to them, nonsense in the night, until they left and went inside to dance or sing karaoke or get another drink. The runners in dresses wished her a happy birthday, bought her shots. She was cut off at the bar, but she didn't care. They held court on the back patio, the younger people ignoring them as much as they could, their friends having as much fun as they were.

At some point she got up and pulled him by the hand, both giggling, to a dark alley that led to the street. There were mop buckets and ladders and hoses, the peripherals of managing a bar with an outdoor patio, standing against the wall in the dark. A tall wooden fence blocked the view to the street and the trash cans, and if you went far enough back you couldn't see the patio.

She pushed him against the wall, aggressive as that frat boy inside of her, kissing him and pushing up his dress. He kissed back, grabbing her head in both hands through her hair, gently but firmly. She slid down and pulled his dick out of his underwear, squatting in front of him, taking him in her mouth and coaxing him to be hard. She was good at it, and he told her so, and she raised an eyebrow and kept going, sloppy and drunk as they both were. He leaned against the wall and closed his eyes.

Usually when he was this drunk there'd be nothing going on down there. But they'd basically been in foreplay for the last three or four hours, and she was really good at what she was doing. Plus the thrill of being discovered – if someone walked out the side door to take out the trash, or came looking for them, or had the same idea she'd had of making this little dark area their personal boudoir. He moaned as she swallowed the tip of his cock in the back of her throat and cupped his balls in her hands. When he thought he couldn't take it anymore, he pulled her off of him and stood her up on her feet, still messy, still drunk, still sloppy.

"I don't want to cum there," he whispered, kissing her. She grinned.

They were both clawing at her dress, bringing it up over her hips. He reached between her naked legs to feel her pussy, wet, ready, like her mouth, her thighs sticky with sweat, the sweet smell of her all over his fingers when he brought them back to his mouth. He licked her off of them, then sent them back to finger her, rubbing her clit, pushing a finger inside her, using his other hand to grab her ass. She threw a leg over his hip, opening herself to him. He kissed her mouth again, laughing, both of them, trying to be quiet, the music from the karaoke bar thumping behind their heads, the loud chit chat from the patio just steps away in the light.

When he pushed himself into her she gasped, moaned, slid herself up to the hilt of his cock. She breathed into his neck, gasping, kissing, pasting her hands to the side of the building on either side of his head. He grabbed her ass and pushed into her, held her there, watched her face move in ecstasy when she threw back her head.

They knocked over a broom and it came down with a loud clatter. They both giggled, hoping no one had heard, standing awkwardly with his cock inside her, her dress falling over both their legs, him pinned against the wall.

She pulled him out, stumbled a bit, leaned back in.

"Let's go home," she whispered.

He nodded and followed her out the side of the side patio through a gate, into the night, without saying goodbye to their friends. Before they struck out he pulled her in and kissed her again.

"Happy birthday," he said, and she laughed and held his hand.

MMF

I was surprised when Nathan told me he was interested in a threesome. The threesome wasn't the part that surprised me; it's that he fantasized about a male-male-female threesome. He'd piqued my curiosity. We were sitting in a candlelit bubble bath in my huge jetted tub after a vigorous, messy, multiorgasmic hour in my bed after dinner. He liked watching porn with threesomes, he said. I said something about, what, he'd like to do double penetration with me, maybe, and he shook his head.

"No," he said, "I think I'd really get off with another man penetrating me while I fucked a woman." He gave a slight shrug and a shy, boyish smile. His brown eyes weren't looking for approval.

He was just sharing intimate information with me. It tickled me.

I'm not sure what my face looked like, but I was actually pleased to hear him say something like that. It was refreshing. Different. So many of the men I'd been with recently had insisted they were "dominant", which meant that they needed to hold a woman down or insist on giving orders during sex. They often said that they would love to have two women together in bed -- more women to obey more orders, of course. But not another man in the bedroom. And their interest in anal sex was usually about inflicting it on a woman, maybe finding ways for her to enjoy it, but not always, it seemed.

Nathan and I had slept together exactly three times when we'd had this conversation. We were both going through major relationship separations and our chemistry was out of this world. We'd agreed neither of us wanted a serious relationship -- just fun times, good conversation, and mind-blowing sex when we could have it. I was seeing other men -- several, in fact -- and he was seeing other women. We'd agreed to a sort of don't ask, don't tell policy about who else we were seeing and when.

I put the information on his desires in my back pocket, so to speak, and continued with our conversation, which ranged from sex to psychology, philosophy, childhood trauma, music, and even skateboarding (his recent obsession, which was why he was ripped with a six pack in spite of being 43 years old and living off a diet of cookies and protein bars). I let my hands trail along his dark, toned legs; I loved stroking the dark fuzz that covered his arms and back, even though he was self-conscious about it. To me, every inch of him was electric. My pussy was constantly wet when he was around. Whenever he left me, I'd take out my vibrator and relive the last time we'd been together until I could see him again.

The next afternoon he sent me a video. It was a well-directed porn. "This reminds me of us yesterday," he texted. I laughed. I'd already watched that video several times -- I'd come back to it over and over because it was exactly what I wanted.

"It's my favorite," I texted back. "Maybe sometime we can watch some of the porn you like."

He sent a thumbs up.

In the back of my mind, I was wondering if I could arrange a threesome for him with any of the men I was seeing. But again, so many of them seemed that they would be offended if I even brought up the idea. There was the one guy who was into bondage and wanted to worship my feet. But he traveled too much and honestly, he wasn't as hot as Nathan, anyway. I wanted a matching set, I laughed to myself.

Then I remembered Peter.

I'd known Peter before I was married. He was a distance runner and there had been rumors he would be trying out for the Olympics. He was an Adonis -- sandy blond, curly hair, green eyes, tan and hairless and cut from marble. A little taller than me and Nathan. But a perfect, sleekly golden match to Nathan's swarthy, hairy-chested skateboarder physique.

Peter and I had engaged in a no strings attached fling over a number of years when I was going through a different break up. We'd call or text when one of us was free. We never went on a date or even had a meal or coffee together. We never met each other's friends. I had taken to calling him "Rock" to my friends, which was what his name meant, because that was what his body was like -- hard. Everywhere. He was a few years younger than me and always ready to go, probably because he ran all the time and didn't drink alcohol or caffeine. Our sex was fantastic and simple. Our conversation was easy. But it was also easy to let go of.

I shivered at the thought of having them both in my bed with me, and giving them both pleasure.

The only problem was I'd deleted Peter's number when I started dating my now ex-husband. As far as I knew, he didn't have social media -- or at least, he hadn't when we had been seeing each other. Not that I'd looked, except sometimes when I was in a certain mood and felt like I'd like to see pictures of him to remember how hot our sex was. I'd never been able to find him online. Just a LinkedIn profile with a tiny thumbnail of him in a suit. Nothing worth touching myself over.

But this time when I Googled him, I found an article about his attempts at Olympic trials which ended by listing his Instagram handle. So I followed him and went back to whatever else was occupying my time between my next date or romp.

Later that evening, after an acceptable period of time for him to get off work, I got a notification that Peter had followed me back on Instagram. Soon after that, I got a message.

"?"

I laughed. That had been our way of instigating a booty call, asking if the other was up, or available. I looked at my watch. It wasn't even 6pm.

"Been a while," I wrote back.

"Didn't think you were free," he responded.

"Recent changes." I sent the message and went back to making dinner.

"So are you asking me over?" he said. He was impatient. Hungry. I loved that.

"Sure," I said. "If you're free."

Within an hour I'd finished my dinner and he was at my house, a new address, a half-hour drive from where he lived. He must have remembered how good our sex was and missed it. Maybe more than I had.

When we were finished, lying in bed, me stroking his bare golden chest while he ran his fingers gently through my strawberry blond hair, I said, "I have a proposition."

"I'm listening," he said, calmly, curiously.

"Have you ever thought about having a threesome?"

He sat up and looked at me with a wide grin on his face. "Sure," he said.

"How about with another man?"

I'd planted the seed at least. I didn't want to plan anything, because I didn't want it to be forced. But I knew both of them were open to the idea. I'd used it as dirty talk with Peter and watched some porn with Nathan. I'd warmed them up to anal play by bringing a metal wand into the bedroom, letting them use it on me, but also using it on them to give them each explosive prostate orgasms. "Imagine if that was another man's cock inside of you," I'd said to Nathan as he came once, his face contorted into wild ecstasy. It was on their minds if nothing else.

So I don't think either of them was surprised when I invited them both over late one Saturday night after I'd been out drinking with some of my girlfriends. I didn't tell either of them that I'd invited them both, but they figured it out pretty quickly. Nathan showed up first and couldn't keep his hands off me in my silk robe as he pushed his way in through the front door. Peter found us there, Nathan's hands all over my ass and lips all over my mouth, hungry for me like always.

He stopped kissing me and looked at the blond man standing on the front porch. Peter looked back at him. Nathan looked at me, somewhat quizzically, and I gave him a little smirk. Peter took another beat, then walked the rest of the way to the door, pushed us gently to go inside, and closed the door behind us.

Neither of them said anything, but they took turns kissing me and pulling off clothes while we stumbled into my bedroom. Nathan kicked off his shoes and untied my robe and Peter pushed it off my shoulders, then bent over to suck on one of my nipples while he undid his belt. Nathan took off his shirt and kissed me again, using both hands to pull my face to his. Peter was unzipping Nathan's fly. We were finally in my bedroom and Peter pushed me onto the bed while he finished taking off his pants and shirt and underwear.

Then he turned to Nathan, who had just finished taking off his shorts and was standing in his socks, and started kissing him. They were both good kissers, I knew. They were well suited to each other -- similar ropy bodies, both tan and hard. It was really, really hot. I pulled my vibrator out of my nightstand drawer, turned it on, and started rubbing it against my clit while I enjoyed the show.

"Oh yeah?" Nathan said to me when he heard the gentle buzzing of the vibe. He had to pull his lips away from Peter, whose mouth sought his neck and chest. "Enjoying the view, I see?" I couldn't help but giggle a little bit, watching Nathan enjoy having Peter all over him. He had his dark fingers in Peter's curly hair, and he moaned as Peter took his cock in his mouth.

I was impressed at how well Peter could suck a dick -- I knew he was good with his mouth, but I hadn't considered the skill would extend from eating pussy to sucking a cock. I hadn't asked if he'd been with a man before. Maybe he just knew how to do it from what he liked.

Nathan couldn't handle it for too long, although he let Peter stroke his shaft and suck on the tip of his cock long enough for me to get very, very close to an orgasm. They both knew the sounds I made before I got off, and Peter stopped and stood up to look at me. Nathan pushed past him onto the bed, took my vibrator out of my hand, and buried his face between my thighs. I was so close already, but he knew exactly how to tease me.

Peter laid next to me and I stroked his cock while Nathan started licking my clit slowly at first, taking me down from the edge. I knew his face would be covered with my slick wetness and there was no way I would last long. Peter leaned in and started kissing me, my mouth, my neck, my breasts. It was hard to concentrate with my hand on his shaft, but he didn't seem to mind my distraction. Nathan was watching me, enjoying how close to the edge I was getting. He slid two fingers inside of me and kept licking diligently, faster and faster. I grabbed Nathan's hair with both hands and rocked my pussy against him, and gasped out a quiet scream while I came all over his tongue.

This drove him absolutely wild. Nathan loved to fuck my pussy right after I came. He got up and went to find a condom in the nightstand, as well as the lube. Panting and still spasming, I sat up and got on my hands and knees over Peter. I looked him in the eye as I took his cock in my hand and stroked it up and down a few times, then started licking the tip.

"I love your blowjobs," he told me, pulling my hair up out of my face and holding it at the crown of my head. I nodded and smiled around his cock, sliding my tongue down the underside while my hand slid the spit all the way down to his balls. I took him deep in the back of my throat when Nathan entered me from behind.

"Fuck you're wet," Nathan said, pushing his enormous cock into my tiny but ready pussy. He started slow, trying not to ruin my concentration on Peter's blowjob. I spit on the head of his cock and went back to sucking on him. He threw his head back in pleasure and Nathan couldn't help but moan slightly, too. I couldn't see his face but I knew he was enjoying the show. I grabbed Peter's balls in my right hand and deep throated him, sucking the tip of his cock in the back of my throat.

Nathan started getting into a rhythm now. Both men were making noises that let me know they were deep in the throes of pleasure. This turned me on even more. My pussy was pulsing on Nathan's cock, throbbing and pulling on him. Peter's cock was responsive to my tongue and mouth, wet with my spit. Finally he stopped me.

"Not yet," he said, breathing heavily. Nathan stopped thrusting for a moment too. Peter got up and found the condoms.

Nathan turned me over to fuck me missionary style, which was his favorite so he could look in my eyes when he or I came. He would usually get close to an orgasm, then wait until I was close enough to cum with him. It was extremely hot, and something I wished Peter knew how to do, although I'd never say that to him.

Nathan handed me my vibrator and encouraged me to put it back on my clit, then slid back into me and started thrusting slowly. We were both watching Peter as he slid on a condom and added extra lube. He brought the bottle behind Nathan and rubbed the darker man's ass. They leaned into each other, kissing, Nathan's cock still buried in my pussy.

Peter trailed his hand down Nathan's body and I watched the look on Nathan's face as he put a finger in his ass. He kept thrusting into me and kissing Peter, his eyes closed but his lips curling into a smile. Watching both of their hard bodies was insanely erotic for me. I pushed my vibrator to a higher speed and held it against my clit, feeling the sensation in a rhythm with Nathan's thrusting.

After a few more minutes, Peter entered Nathan fully with his cock. Nathan was looking me in the eye and his face took on that contorted look of pleasure that I loved so much. Peter let Nathan's thrusting into me direct how much he entered Nathan at first. Nathan was holding himself up over me so I could reach my clit with my vibrator, and Peter was holding both my legs.

"Fuck, wow," Nathan said. He couldn't help himself. He was overwhelmed with pleasure.

I saw Peter start thrusting harder. He was enjoying watching me get off, too, I knew. He loved it when I played with my vibrator while he was inside me. I wondered if he could feel it through Nathan now, too.

It didn't take long for me to get back to the edge, and I threw my head back and gasped as another orgasm wracked my body. Nathan looked me in the eye and held his cock inside of me while I pulsed over him. He was grabbing my shoulders hard, and Peter was thrusting hard into him too. Finally he couldn't take it anymore either, and I felt him shudder inside of me as he released the hardest orgasm I'd ever seen him have. I stared into his eyes as he throbbed, his face contorted in the way I loved, Peter still thrusting behind him.

Nathan collapsed on top of me and Peter laughed a bit. He pulled his cock out of Nathan's ass and came and stood next to the bed where I was lying, gasping and panting for air. He pulled the condom off, put some more lube on his cock, and put my hand on it.

I finished him with a sloppy hand job. Nathan sat up to watch as Peter roped onto my chest, another astonishing orgasm after so much stimulation. I loved the noises Peter made when he came, grunting and gasping. I knew I'd remember this night for the rest of my life.

We lay in bed for a while -- Nathan on my right, Peter on my left, limbs tangled and sweaty, cooling off under the fan. I fell asleep at some point, and when I woke up, both men were gone. But I was sure we'd probably see each other again soon.

Under the Mimosa Tree

It was hot. It was only late May and already it felt like the hottest day of late August – 102 degrees all day. It was also after 10pm and even with the sun set and a breeze blowing through the thick air, sweat was gathering at the corners of Nick's knees, soaking the back of his tee shirt and the edges of his shorts. He and Melissa were sitting on her back patio, outside, sipping on last beers and saying a long farewell. She was leaving the next day. Her packed car was just feet away, ready for a six-hour drive to a west Texas writers retreat.

"You're just going to leave me here, alone, for three months," he said again, a little calmer than when he'd exclaimed it to her three weeks ago when she'd announced she'd gotten into the program.

"Two and a half months," she corrected him, just as she had that first time, wiping her mouth from the swig of the Lone Star bottle she'd just taken. "I'll be back before Labor Day. We can go fishing."

He wanted to be happy for her. This was a big opportunity for her. But he was scared of the time without her, where his mind would wander.

"What am I going to do without you," he said, quietly, more to himself than to her, taking a swig from his own sweating bottle.

"You'll be fine," she said, leaning over her knees, which were tucked under her chin in the blue plastic patio chair, to hit him lightly on his own knee. "It's not like I won't be in touch. I can still text from west Texas."

He had a mild panic in his gut, though, at being left behind. She'd become his best friend in the quick six months they'd known each other. She'd helped him through a break up, not by being a rebound, but just by listening. Melissa was always listening. She never gave advice, either, not really. She just listened and maybe would suggest an article she'd read about that feeling he had; or a song she knew that reminded her of that feeling herself; a validation from somewhere. Or she just said, "I'm sorry. That sucks."

But they'd also become activity partners, doing everything together. She'd encouraged him to dig out and fix up his old bike so they could ride around town together, grabbing drinks with their mutual friends, watching sunsets, catching free concerts in the spring before it was too hot. She'd made him go to the library with her and renew his library card and check out books. He'd quit reading in his last relationship, and now he was reading again.

He hadn't thought about dating, though she'd suggested it. He couldn't go on the apps. His other friends were all in relationships. He'd be the third wheel now, single and unhappy.

He had a lump in his throat. What would he do without her? He cleared his throat and drank some more. She was nursing her beer since she had to leave early for the drive, but he was on his third. He'd come over to see her off on her last night. She was exhausted but had agreed to one more porch hang. They were listening to music on her little Bluetooth speaker from his phone, his new favorite album of the spring. It was soft and melodic, a little sad for this kind of heat, but it echoed how he felt.

The mimosa tree in her yard was in full bloom, loud and exuberant, announcing its fecundity with a heady scent that was intoxicating. There was still some jasmine blooming on the fence behind them, too. These were his favorite smells – the springtime in central Texas, tapping you lightly on the face whenever you got distracted by the impending heat, making you dizzy with the promise of spring and fun and youth.

"You smell it, too," Melissa said, bringing him back from his reverie in the scent. "That mimosa tree is magnificent."

"It really is," Nick said, another swig from his beer going down.

"Let's go lay in the hammock," Melissa suggested, putting her beer bottle on the table – still half full – and standing up. She held her hand out to him and lifted him out of his own chair. He finished his beer and let his bottle join hers on the glass top. He followed her down the quick steps to the hammock under the mimosa tree.

The moon was a thin sliver over her house, and surely, she could name all the stars overhead if they'd been in a place to see them. But the mimosa tree kept the sky at bay, as well as half the street that wasn't blocked by the tall fence of her backyard. It was dark on this side of the house, although none of the windows really looked out over the hammock under the mimosa tree. Still, he wondered if her roommate was out or had gone to bed.

The hammock was wide and sturdy, attached to a stand rather than a tree. It was padded instead of a rope, so it was more like a hanging couch than a traditional hammock. It easily held both of their bodies, with no fear of falling out on either side. They lay side by side, their shoulders touching, staring into the leaves and flowers swaying gently in the breeze overhead. A streetlight was just close enough to give ambient lighting, but not enough to make out anything specific. Once in a while a firefly lit up.

"What will you write about?" he asked her, lamely.

"The human condition," she said, not missing a beat.

"Right," he said. "Of course."

She laughed, a light bell that rang in his ears. It tickled him down his neck and spine. He loved her laugh.

"I've been working on some stuff," she said. "Short stories. I'm hoping to get them workshopped. Get some new perspective on them. I'm stuck with the ending on one."

"What's it about?" he asked.

She sighed. "Werewolves," she said.

He almost choked on his laugh. "Werewolves?"

"Yes," she said, flicking him lightly on the shoulder. "It's a story about coming to terms with your inner monster."

"Okay," he said. He felt the beer hitting him just a little. He wasn't a lightweight, but he'd lost some weight during the breakup over the winter and three beers hit him harder than they used to in college, a mere three years ago. "I've never read anything you've written."

"I'll send you the werewolf story," she said, "once it's in a better place."

"You can send it to me now," he said.

"It's pretty rough," she said.

He took a beat and a breath.

"Did you know I studied literature?"

"You what?" He could feel her turning toward him a little. He just looked straight up. "Like, in college?"

"Yeah," he said. "I thought about being a comparative lit major."

"Wow," she said. "My high school English teacher told me to do that. He said the smartest people he knew were comp lit majors." I know, he thought, you've told me. "What was the other language you were going to compare with?"

"It's not always comparing languages," he told her. He knew she'd studied French and was an adept writer in that and English. "I was thinking about film and literature. But I really wasn't very good with either."

"So why would I want you to read my rough draft?" she laughed, the bell, again.

"At least I'd be better than your average Joe off the street, I guess," he chuckled back. "I can pick out themes. Tone. Foreshadowing. The important stuff."

He could feel her smiling next to him. The air under the hammock was keeping them cooler than the plastic chairs on the patio, but he could feel her heat still through her thin white tank top and shorts.

"Ok, I'll send you the rough draft," she said.

They listened to the breeze and the bugs and the night birds. A neighbor a block or two away was having a party, music thumping vaguely over voices in the backyard.

"What am I going to do without you," he muttered again, bringing his hands back from behind his head and laying them flat beside him.

"That's the third time you've said that this week," she said. She slid her right hand into his left and held it there. "I promise you'll be ok. I'll be ok. I'll be back in the blink of an eye. And I'll write you all the time. And text you. And call you. It'll be just like I'm here."

He shook his head slightly. "No, it won't."

She squeezed his hand. He felt a swell of courage, from the sweet smell of the mimosa and the softness of her skin mixed with the firm way she held his hand. He leaned up on his left elbow and looked her in the face, her big dark eyes, the tip of her nose, the swell of her lips. He knew them all, even though they were so new to him still.

She met his gaze, her eyes focusing on his face under the tree branches.

"What," she said.

He shrugged a little. Maybe she was going to ruin the moment. Maybe she didn't want this the way he did. They sat looking at each other for a moment, taking in the late spring, the early heat wave, their young faces, the speed at which they'd gotten to know each other, but still the way they felt utterly familiar. He knew she felt the same. She must. But he was stuck here, looking.

And in an instant she reached a hand behind his neck and brought his face to hers and kissed him. He kissed back. She was sweaty from the heat and a day of packing, but she smelled delicious, a compliment to the jasmine and the mimosa, a musk that made her mouth seem irresistible to him. He was gentle, not trying to rush anything. Just a kiss, that was enough, he thought.

But she was hungrier than him. She ran her hands through his thick hair, grabbing at the base of his skull, pulling him into her, breathing heavily into the beer soaked kisses. She breathed into his ear while he kissed her neck, both of them raising goosebumps on each other's skin.

Somehow, even though she was so much smaller than him, she turned him over and pinned him in the swaying hammock, slipping her tank top off in one quick motion, her small breasts fully visible now, rather than barely hidden by the thin material. He had tried not to look before. But now he reached up and took them both in his hands. Her skin was so soft, a little damp, a little sticky.

Somehow she wiggled out of her shorts, too, and then she was naked over him, straddling him, fully clothed still. And he just looked at her. She looked back at him. She smiled, knowingly, and leaned back in to kiss him, her long dark hair falling over both of them. Usually he would be self conscious about people watching from the street. But he didn't care tonight. She was beautiful. If people wanted to watch and they could see anything, let them watch.

She kept kissing him – she was a really good kisser, firm in the right places, soft in the right places, just aggressive enough but making it a conversation rather than a demand or a script –

while she deftly reached for his fly. She could feel that he was hard under his jean shorts, which were too heavy and hard for this kind of weather, but they were all he ever wore in the summer. She ran a hand over his cock, through the jeans, before unbuttoning and unzipping the fly. She pulled him out of his boxers and started stroking him.

"Oh, hello," she said, giggling quietly.

"Hi," he replied, taking his turn to hold her head and bring her in for another kiss. He pulled away briefly and licked his thumb, then found her clit and strummed it gently.

She moaned, trying to be quiet, and sat up straight, pushing her hair back from her face with her free hand, stroking him still with her other. He applied more pressure with his thumb, moving in small circles under the small shock of hair. He let his fingers wander some more and found her wetness not far from where his thumb was working.

She sat up with her eyes closed for another few moments, letting him stroke her, pulling gently on his cock, breathing in more and more heavily. And then in one swift motion she pulled him inside of her, tight and pulsing and wet and as hot as the night around them.

He put his other hand behind his head and kept stroking her clit with his thumb, the wetness from her pussy now spreading over his cock and everywhere. It took a bit to get him fully inside her, but he let her take control. He was afraid to move, for fear she'd disappear and this would just be a dream.

Once she got him fully inside of her, she rode him gently, rocking back and forth with her hips, the hammock still sturdy but swaying. He was enjoying the show, her fully naked body above him, enjoying herself with his body while he stroked her clit and gave her pleasure. This was his favorite.

Her breathing started to get more and more shallow, her hip rocking less and less controlled, her moaning turning into sharp gasps between coos. He knew she was going to cum, and he watched intently as she approached the inevitable. Finally she put both hands on his shoulders and bucked against him, her pussy throbbing with his cock inside of her, her thighs shaking, her body quaking over him. It was so hot, he couldn't stop himself. He thought briefly of making her cum again, but his body was ready to give up, and she milked the cum out of him, squeezing him over and over as he gasped himself.

She fell on top of him, spent, their chests heaving against each other, the sweat and the heat and the mimosa and the jasmine and the party in the distance coming back into focus. Some bro yelled, "Woo!" and they both burst out laughing.

She reassembled herself next to him, cuddled up, a little chilly now as she was naked in the breeze.

He cradled her body, her head on his chest, breathing together.

"What am I going to do without you," she whispered. He kissed the top of her head.

"You'll come back," he said.

She nodded.

"I'll be here waiting," he said. She nodded again.

They dozed off in the heat, just for a bit, just to keep the inevitable morning at bay a little longer.

A Flat Tire in the Rain

Samantha had just gotten off work when the rain started. It had been a cruddy night at the diner, maybe because of the cold, but there had been virtually no customers, and so she'd basically stood around from her shift's start at 6pm until she got off at 2am. She was tired, her feet hurt, and it was raining hard, so hard she didn't see the giant branch in the road until it was too late. And now it was 2:15 in the morning, she was alone on the road, and she had a flat tire.

Just to make matters worse, her cell phone was out of batteries. Samantha liked to think of herself as the kind of girl who was self-reliant, but even after 10 years of driving, she didn't know how to change a tire. She wanted to sit down and cry. But instead, she opened the trunk of her Toyota 4Runner and started digging for the jack and the spare.

A light came up behind her, and she was a little afraid that the passing car would splash dirty muddy water onto her as it passed. She was even more frightened when she realized the car had stopped behind her own and someone was getting out. She turned when she heard the car door slam. The owner had left the lights on, and she was blinded as the driver approached.

"Need help?" said a man's voice. Now Samantha was terrified. She swallowed.

"Well," she said, "actually, yes, I do."

She had just been telling her sister yesterday that people needed to trust each other more. Still, it was past 2 in the morning, she was a woman, and she was alone. She held the jack in her hands just in case.

The man stepped into the light so that he blocked it from Samantha's eyes. She got a good look at him and she was less afraid. He was a young guy, medium build, dark-skinned with a hat on. He looked friendly enough.

"These trucks can be tricky," he said. "It's a bad night to be out."

Samantha nodded. "It's been a bad night all around," she said.

He looked in the back of her truck and noticed her squinting in the light. "Oh, sorry about the lights," he said. "I was actually kind of… afraid." He shrugged and smiled. His innocence was disarming.

"I can understand that," Samantha said. She turned to the trunk of her 4Runner. "I found the jack," she said. She held it up. "Not that I know how to use it."

"Aha," said the man. "Okay. The spare should be under the rug here…" He lifted the rug and the tire was there.

"Perfect," Samantha said. She looked at him. "And now what?"

He laughed a little. "I'll do it," he said. "I've done this a trillion times." He took the jack from her and went to work. She noticed his muscles under his jacket as he worked. She'd always been a sucker for nice shoulders. She hadn't been with a guy in a long time, not since her boyfriend had left a few months ago. For that slimy whore, she thought to herself. She shuddered a little. The man changing the tire noticed.

"Cold?" he asked.

"Oh, no, I'm fine," Samantha said. It was a bit chilly, being the middle of October, and their breaths showed in steam trails as they spoke. She watched him as he pumped the jack up under her car, his arms working methodically. She shivered again, but not because she was cold or angry this time.

"I'm Samantha," she said.

"Tom," he answered. He held his right hand out and she took it. It was warm and dry and his handshake was firm. He had thick fingers and she liked how they felt. "You have really soft hands," he said, and then she saw that he was blushing.

"Thank you," she answered. She gave him her best smile. She watched him work, trying to stay out of his light, watching him work.

"Is there a lug wrench?" he asked. "I need to loosen these nuts before I put the car too high up."

I'd like to loosen your nuts, Samantha found herself thinking. She leaned into the trunk and looked for a wrench.

"This thing?" she asked, holding the long tool out for him.

"That's it," he said. She approached and handed it to him, wishing she could find a way for their fingers to brush.

He took the tool from her and loosened the lug nuts one at a time, then finished jacking the car up. He removed the lug nuts the rest of the way.

"You make this look so easy," Samantha said.

Tom shrugged. "It kind of is easy," he said. "I mean, once you've done it as many times as I have."

"Do you work for a shop or something?" Samantha asked.

"No, actually," Tom said, removing the tire and putting it on the ground. "I'm an accountant."

"An accountant?" she said. That was boring. And stable. She loved boring and stable. Frantically Samantha found herself searching his left hand for a wedding ring. She found none. "So, Tom, are you single?"

He looked up at her, somewhat confused. "Actually, yes," he said. He stood up. "I need the spare now," he said.

Samantha beat him to the back of the truck to get it. The back of the truck was higher than the front, up on the jack, and inside the trunk it was warm and dry. She lifted the spare out and held it in front of her. Tom stood in the rain, looking at her curiously. He reached for the spare. She gave it over slowly, but leaned in while he took it and kissed him softly on the lips.

He pulled away slowly and studied her for a moment, the spare tire in his hands. He put it down on the ground next to the jack. For a moment she thought he was going to go back to the work, or, worse, leave. But the next second he had taken her by the shoulders and was kissing her back.

Tom was a great kisser and it felt good to be touching him. He was strong and gentle and he tasted sweet. She was hungry for him. Before she knew it, he had lifted her into the back of the truck and they were peeling their wet clothes off. He smelled great, and it made her want him even more.

Soon enough they were naked, and he had a hand on one of her large breasts. He was hard and his cock was big in her hands. She stroked him while he kissed her neck, then his mouth found one of her nipples. She had always had sensitive nipples and she gasped a little as he sucked on them.

"You okay?" he asked.

"Don't stop," she moaned. He went back to her breasts and she stroked him gently, then harder as he sucked on her nipple harder.

He moved his mouth down her stomach, a trail of soft kisses to her mound. She wished he had hair to grab onto, but under his hat he had a shaved head. It added to his clean look. She pulled on his ears instead as he started licking her vulva. She lay her head back and gritted her teeth together as he found her clit and sucked on it gently. She felt her eyes rolling back in her head. She hadn't felt this good in a long time.

When he slid a finger into her wet pussy, she convulsed into an orgasm and exploded onto him.

"Whoa," he said.

She was gasping for breath. He fingered her slowly as she came all over him, and it took a moment or two for the shivers of pleasure to stop.

When he finally removed his finger, she felt hungry for him still.

"Don't stop," she moaned again.

He sat up and got on his hands and knees over her. "I won't," he said. He was digging in his jeans for something, and then he pulled out a condom and slid it over his hard member.

"You're so good with safety," Samantha laughed. She pulled him down and kissed him. He laughed as she did so.

His cock found her slit and slid in, and she felt the thrill of pleasure again.

"I have to be gentle," he said as she moaned into his ear. "I don't want the jack to slip out."

She shuddered into another orgasm. "Whatever you do seems to be just fine by me," she gasped.

He started thrusting, gentle as ever, and Samantha thought the pleasure would never end. His hand found her breast again, and kneaded it gently. Samantha bit his ear and he pulled away a little, surprised. She laughed. He laughed too, and his hips kept moving.

She pushed herself against him, grinding with his thrusts, and felt her clit touching his mound. She wasn't sure if she would come again, but the feeling was so good she didn't care. She grabbed his ass with both hands and squeezed it, moaning with pleasure.

The moan sent him over the edge. Tom's back tensed up and she could see he was coming. She pulled him in as close as she could and savored his face as he was wracked with orgasm. She thought it might be the only ungentle thing about him.

When they were done they lay in the trunk together listening to the rain patter on the roof. Samantha traced a line down his spine with her finger.

"Do you always give this kind of service to damsels in distress?" she asked with a grin.

"Honestly, no," Tom answered, returning her smile. "You're the first."

"Well," she said, "now I think I owe you for your chivalry. Once we're done with the tire, maybe you can come home with me, and help me with a few projects around the house?"

He studied her face in the dark for a moment. "I think I could handle that," he said.

"Oh," Samantha said, "I definitely think you could, too."

Added Value

Walt had been working on Krystal Fleming's Upper East Side loft for three months. He was just about ready to throw in the towel and tell the fussy debutante to get a new designer for the apartment. She wouldn't agree to anything – not the color scheme, not the furniture, not the paint, not the rugs. Even when she picked through magazines and highlighted her favorites, she'd change her mind by the next day. The only things she readily agreed to do were ones that she thought would add value to the apartment.

"Does that offer me an added value?" she would ask.

He couldn't explain to her that furniture would never add value to an apartment unless they stayed with the apartment. And that there weren't many improvements that could be made on this already-renovated loft. She frustrated him to no end.

True, she was racking up a fortune in hourly costs. But Walt was beginning to fear she wasn't going to pay any of it. He'd heard that interior designers and architects were often left with bills unpaid because of bad clients. And he was afraid Krystal was one such client.

They were supposed to meet at 4pm in her loft today to "chat", as Krystal had said in her text message. That was another thing – she never called, she always texted. Her emails were gratingly short, grammatically incorrect wastes of bandwidth that left Walt with more questions than answers, even if her email was a response to a simple inquiry from Walt.

He was only a few years older than her – six, to be exact. She had just graduated from college, which Walt was sure her dad was a regent or docent or whatever they called huge donors. Walt doubted Krystal had ever gone to classes. As far as he was concerned, Krystal was just a rich girl with daddy's credit card. He almost hated her. He'd worked really hard through college and grad school, with an undergraduate degree in architecture and a graduate degree in design. He'd worked the entire time, too, and had established himself as a young but up-and-coming interior designer in New York. He was the next hot thing, even though he wasn't gay.

Krystal was, of course, late. It was 4:20 already. Luckily, Walt had expected this, since Krystal had never been on time to any of their meetings. He'd scheduled her as the last meeting of the day, so he could just go home afterwards. It had been a long week.

He wandered around the loft a little, running his hands over the modern furniture he'd special ordered for Krystal. The couches were gorgeous, soft red bison leather, custom-built from the French furniture store Roche Bobois. They had cost nearly $20,000 and had taken several weeks to build. The delivery men had had to use the back stairs to get the couch up to the 20$_{th}$-floor loft, because the moving elevator hadn't been big enough. Krystal had looked at the red-leather sectional and shrugged.

"Could you, like, get something else?" she'd asked.

The memory of it made him clinch his fists. He had to tell her he couldn't work with her anymore. He didn't care what kind of billionaire her father was.

Krystal had no taste, and he hadn't seen a dime of her money. He was quitting today.

As soon as she showed up.

At 4:45, when Walt was considering turning on the flat screen TV hanging on the wall in front of the couches and ordering some on-demand pornography, Krystal breezed into the apartment.

"Oh, hey," she said, flinging her Louis Vuitton purse onto the couch next to Walt. The designer flinched. He hoped the hardware on the purse wouldn't scratch the soft red leather of the couch. "I have to pee."

She darted into the restroom down the hall. Walt closed his eyes and rubbed his temples.

He heard the toilet flush and Krystal re-emerged.

"So," she said, "what's up?"

Other than the fact that you're 45 minutes late, and I hate you, nothing, Walt thought. Krystal started rummaging through her purse. She was wearing a set of velour jogging clothes with something written on the ass in glitter, which made it hard not to watch her as she bent over. She was cute, Walt couldn't deny it. Her brown hair with red and gold highlights was up in a ponytail, and she was wearing tasteful gold earrings. She looked rich and careless.

"Just waiting for our meeting," Walt said. Was he nervous? Something was tightening in his throat, and he cleared it.

Krystal quit digging and looked at him over her shoulder. "Oh, yeah, sorry," she said. She went back to her purse. "I got caught up at dad's office."

What a fabulous excuse, Walt thought.

"How is Mr. Fleming?" he asked.

"Fine, for an old dude," Krystal said. She'd found what she wanted and

turned around to face Walt. "Okay, so," she said, holding an envelope out to him.

"Dad said you probably called this meeting because you needed to be paid. So here's a check and stuff."

A check? Walt was dumfounded. They hadn't even sent an invoice yet. He took the envelope from her. "Oh, thank you," he said. It wasn't sealed, so he opened it and pulled the slim but heavy paper out of the fold.

$100,000.

He felt his eyebrows go up.

"Is that enough?" Krystal asked, shifting her weight from one young leg to the other.

"Yes," Walt said. "But we didn't send an invoice."

"Dad said he wanted to pre-empt that or something," Krystal replied. She flipped her hair a little and walked towards the kitchen. "Anyway, he says we need to hold onto you because you're really good and he doesn't want Lindsey Fetterman stealing you away."

Walt chuckled. He stood up and followed her into the kitchen. She was helping herself to a bright red apple. "It doesn't work that way," he said. "I can work on both of your lofts."

"Well, but daddy doesn't want you to think we're cheapos or whatever." She bit into the apple. She chewed loudly for a moment. "So, that's okay then?"

Walt took a deep breath. "Yes," he said. "It's fine."

Guess I won't be quitting, he thought. He looked at the check again. He

could feel Krystal watching him. When he looked up, she took another bite of her apple.

"Ya' sure?" she said over the juice in her mouth.

"Yes," he said. She took a step towards him. He felt his throat tighten up again.

"Because, I can throw in some added value," she said. She unzipped the top of her velour hoodie and put her apple down on the table.

Without a coaster, was Walt's first thought. The juice might ruin the finish. He didn't move anything but his eyes, from the apple back to Krystal. He could see now that she'd almost unzipped her top completely. She wasn't wearing anything under the hoodie.

"Are you gay?" Krystal asked, her head tilted to the side. "Paying more attention to your precious furniture than to me?"

Instead of replying, he grabbed pushed his hands around her waist, under the open hoodie, and loosed her large breasts. They were fake, he knew, and she had no tan lines, even though she had an even, golden tan. Her nails were perfectly manicured, light pink French style, as were her toes in her flip-flops.

Rich girls, he thought. He leaned down and kissed her. She kissed him back, grabbing the hair on the back of his head. I need a haircut, he realized.

Krystal didn't seem to mind. She kissed him harder and wriggled out of her hoodie, letting it fall to the floor. Walt started on her pants. Again, she was wearing no underthings and had no tan lines. She stepped of her flip-flops as her velour pants fell to her ankles. She stepped out of those as well. She had a hard body, fake tits and all, and Walt was glad he'd bought that gym membership a few months ago.

"Let's do it on the couch," she said.

Walt winced, but she was dragging him to the living room, naked and perfect-looking, and he couldn't say no. His cock was hard in his pants and Krystal was already fumbling with his belt. He pulled his sweater over his head with his undershirt. He kicked off his shoes.

There is seriously no way to take off one's pants in a sexy manner, he thought as he unzipped and pulled them off as quickly as possible.

Krystal got down on her knees in front of him on the plush Berber rug. Her tan looked great against the red and black pattern from his point of view as she took his member out of his boxer shorts and started to suck gently.

A tongue piercing, he thought. He smiled to himself and grabbed her ponytail. Rich girls, he thought. He closed his eyes and used her ponytail to guide her mouth on his cock. In and out, slowly, gently, he was surprised at how good she was. Of course, it occurred to her, what else was she going to do with her time in college?

The piercing felt great against the tip of his penis. She knew what she was doing. He didn't want her to stop, but she did after a few moments. She stood up and acted like she was going to kiss him, but he pushed her face down on the couch. She looked over her shoulder at him, smiling, and put her hands on the back of the couch, her knees on the cushions, and stuck her ass out. He slapped it and grabbed her hips.

She was surprisingly tight as he slid in, and unsurprisingly hairless. He wondered how much she spent a month waxing everything. She'd probably had electrolysis, he thought as he started to pound her. She was moaning and leaning into him as he did so. He realized one of her hands wasn't on the back of the couch anymore and was actively moving on her clit.

He started to pound her harder, rocking her back and forth on the couch. The leather felt good on his knees. He wished he'd had the wherewithal to take off his socks and feel the Berber carpet under his feet.

He grabbed onto her ponytail again, giving it a good yank, while he grabbed onto her breast with his other hand and started thrusting closer, deeper, and faster.

She seemed to be really enjoying herself. He could feel her snatch throbbing on his cock and knew she was going to come soon. Her hand moved faster and faster on her clit and was grazing his cock a little as he thrusted.

So glad we're doing this doggy style, he thought. He was sure the wetness from her cunt would ruin the leather on the couch.

She came loudly, and leaned into him as she did so, interrupting his thrusting. He let her enjoy it for a moment and enjoyed the pulsing of her pussy on his cock. Then he pushed her forward again and started up again.

He glanced at the clock on the wall. It was five. Time to quit.

Somehow the thought of this as business made him really hot. He slammed into her two more times, then felt the cum rising in his cock. He burst into her with a short grunt and felt himself rope six, seven times before he was done.

He collapsed against Krystal's perfect back for a second.

"Whew," he said quietly.

"You said it," Krystal agreed.

After he'd gathered his clothes and put his check in his briefcase, he said a short goodbye and headed to the door. Krystal followed him.

"So," she said, playing with her ponytail, still completely naked. She held the door with her right hand and was leaning against it. "Do we need to have another meeting? Tomorrow at 4 maybe?"

Walt looked at his watch.

"You be here at 4," he said, "I'll show up at 4:30. Maybe."

He turned and walked to the elevator with her eyes on his back.

He was glad he hadn't quit after all.

Shopping

Jessica had always loved going to the mall on Saturdays. Sure, it was always crowded, particularly around the holidays, and there were screaming children with horrible mothers and plenty of awful teenagers. But she loved the crowds. And the mall had always given her a feeling of excitement and possibility, ever since she was a pre-teen who had to take the bus to get there. The thought of new clothes and the excitement of seeing people she'd never seen before and would never see again made her very hopeful, no matter how loud and obnoxious the people at the mall could be.

She definitely needed some hope in her life now, after "the break-up". True, she'd only been with the guy for a few months, but somehow, he'd taken her for a real ride. She felt used, ugly, and hopeless.

Their sex life had been miserable, which she knew was his fault, but she felt personally responsible for it nevertheless. Her self-esteem was at a real low and she needed a pick-me-up. The Saturday after they quit speaking to each other, she realized she hadn't been to the mall the entire time they'd been dating. She decided it was just what she needed to pick herself up.

Being a Saturday at 4pm only two weeks away from Christmas, the mall was packed. Every store seemed full of people harassing the salespeople. No one was happy – except for Jessica. This was exactly the distraction she was looking for. There were plenty of young, good-looking boys around – far too young for her, but she could look, couldn't she? And there were a few good-looking girls who caught her attention, too.

Jessica knew she was bisexual, but she always had difficulty finding girls to hook up with. *Probably because I hang out at the mall*, she told herself, strolling slowly through the throngs of people. *Girls who want to have sex with girls probably don't pick each other up at the mall.* The two women she'd slept with had been random hook ups, and she couldn't figure out how to replicate the situations. After this break up, though, she thought she'd be up for a hot night out with anyone, regardless of gender. As long as they knew what they were doing.

Depressed as she was, she could feel a definite throbbing in her nether regions. The heat off the bodies in the mall was actually making her horny. Youth, beauty, hope, heat – all of this made her almost desperate for sex. The extreme Christmas break flirting between the teens and pre-teens here wasn't helping her at all. She allowed herself a short fantasy about a young guy working at a video game store. She paused for a moment to watch him through the front of the window. She stood outside, pretending to be interested in the store's display of the latest gaming console. He was probably 17, maybe 18, half her age at most, and he was probably just a little shy, judging by the look on his face as he helped the older woman before him. He was tall for his age, and he had nice, lean muscles. His hair was dark and he had dark eyes and perfect olive skin. She imagined grabbing him by the hair on the back of his head and kissing him wildly. He'd be surprised at first, but then give in, and eventually she'd lead his hand under her skirt…

Smiling, she walked on, even hotter and more desperate than before. She was going through the Rolodex of men she knew in her mind, wondering if any of them would be interested in a Saturday evening roll in the hay. She'd been out of contact with most of them since dating this last guy and wondered if it would be too cheesy to call them so soon.

She came across the over-priced lingerie store she'd always loved visiting, filled to the brim with women from ages 12 to 95. The store took up three mall stores in itself, with a pre-teen section full of pinks and blues, as well as a section full of lotions and perfumes that made Jessica's head hurt. The center section was more mature, with the adult pieces that made the store's catalogs famous for men to jack off to. Jessica decided to buy herself something sexy. She was in a sexy mood anyway.

Most of the racks in the center section looked like a bomb had hit them. The bras and panties were completely out of color and size order, and were either barely hanging on their hangers, hanging sideways, or falling on the floor. The salesgirls (and they were all girls) seemed harried and ready to snap. There were dozens of them, dressed in all black and wandering around offering help to the demanding women throughout the store.

Jessica started digging through the debris, looking for something very sexy, and maybe over the top. A corset, she decided, would be perfect, with some cheeky matching panties, and a pair of thigh highs with seams down the back. And a new satin robe if she could find one. But looking around her, the task of finding these items seemed rather impossible.

"Can I help you?"

Jessica turned around to a young salesgirl – probably in her early 20s, with short, spiky hair and bright green eyes. She was taller than Jessica, and slim, with high breasts and slim hips

"I'm looking for something really sexy," Jessica said, oozing confidence. She'd already decided she was attracted to this girl and might treat herself to another fantasy after they were done.

"You've come to the right place," the salesgirl responded. She smiled. She had a gap between her front teeth, and Jessica imagined running her tongue over it.

Jessica smiled back and nodded. "Specifically, a corset, matching panties, and thigh highs with a seam. Oh, and a robe."

"I think we can manage that," the girl said. "Do you have any specific colors in mind?"

Jessica mulled this over a moment. "Just show me what you've got," she said.

The salesgirl led her to a quieter corner at the very back of the adult women's store, where, judging by the quality of the garments, everything was much more expensive and therefore out of reach for most of the mall-shopping population. Only one other salesgirl had a client in the area with her. The clothes here were much less disorganized, and it felt as if Jessica had been led into an oasis.

"This is our exclusive line of silk lingerie," the salesgirl was explaining. Jessica took a look at her name tag. Tanya, it said. "Everything here is hand sewn in Italy, and we also do tailoring if it doesn't fit you exactly."

Jessica ran her hand over a pair of red silk panties. They were so smooth and soft. She felt her clitoris twitch.

"I like the red here," Jessica said. "Do you have any matching corsets?"

"Of course," Tanya answered. She led Jessica to a rack of several corsets in different colors. "Silk, again," Tanya explained as Jessica ran her hand over the front of the boning. "What's your size?"

"I'm a 36C," Jessica said. Tanya sorted through the corsets and pulled out a red one, shining in the soft light.

"36C," she echoed.

Jessica took the edge of the corset in her hand and rubbed it between her fingers.

"Would you like to try it on?" Tanya said. "I can grab you the panties, too. I think I can guess your size."

"Sure," Jessica said.

"And a robe, too," Tanya went on. She took Jessica back into a quiet dressing room – this section of the store even had its own corner of exclusive dressing rooms – and left her with the corset. The rooms didn't have doors, Jessica noted. Privacy was achieved through thick black curtains, just like in the dressing rooms on the other, less-exclusive sides of the store, which Jessica had visited often. This room was larger than the others she'd seen, and had a small plush chair upholstered in red velvet – much better than the terrible plastic stools Jessica knew took up the other dressing rooms.

Jessica took all her clothes off, except her heels, to make herself feel taller, and stood in front of the mirror admiring her body. It was great for any age, and though she was in her 30s, she knew she was as sexy as any teenager. Her breasts were large but still perky, and she had a rather perfect stomach. Her blonde hair was loose and went down her back. She had ample hips and a great ass and loved her calves. She smiled at herself. She knew she was gorgeous, stupid ex-boyfriend or no.

She undid all the hook-and-eye closures on the corset. She was going to take her time trying this on and savor it.

A hand popped through the curtain holding a pair of red silk panties on a hanger.

"Here are the panties," Tanya said.

"Thanks," Jessica replied, taking them from her. The hand disappeared through the dark folds.

"Be right back with the robe."

Jessica slid the panties on, being careful not to snag the silk on her black pumps. In spite of the security strip over the crotch, they fit perfectly.

Tanya did know her sizes after all. The silk felt divine against Jessica's skin. She started hooking the corset back together over her chest but couldn't reach all the way back to the middle hooks. It felt like it was going to fit, but if she couldn't do the hooks all the way, she'd never know.

She stopped trying and decided to wait for Tanya to return so the sales girl could help her finish the hooks.

Jessica looked at herself in the mirror again and grinned. She allowed herself to imagine Tanya coming into the dressing room to help. Jessica would hold her hair up while Tanya started helping her with the hooks. Then Jessica would reach one hand back and touch Tanya on the hip. The girl would stop hooking, and Jessica would turn around. They'd lock lips and Jessica would unzip the girl's pants and start touching her, over her panties at first…

Jessica found herself pushing her own hand down into the red silk panties she was wearing. She found her clitoris, hot and throbbing, and started touching herself. She hadn't masturbated in so long, it felt juicy and wonderful, even standing up.

"Here's the robe," Tanya said, coming in through the curtain.

She'd caught Jessica literally red-handed.

The two women looked at each other for a long moment. Jessica didn't move her hand. Her heart was pounding. Tanya had a funny look on her face, holding the red silk robe before her. She cocked an eyebrow. Jessica was at a loss for words. She could pull her hand out and pretend nothing had happened, or... or what?

After what seemed like an eternity, Tanya dropped the robe to the ground and lunged forward. She put her hand on the back of the older woman's head and pulled her in for a long, wet kiss. Jessica kissed back, surprised but pleased. She pulled her hand out of her panties and ran her tongue over Tanya's teeth, just as she'd imagined. They were slick and smooth, like pearls. Jessica felt Tanya's hands groping her ass fervently.

Then Tanya pushed Jessica to the floor gently and laid her out on top of the silk she'd dropped. It was cool on her back as the salesgirl kissed her neck and shoulders. Jessica's heart was pounding wildly. She was trying to touch Tanya wherever she could, but the thin, tall girl was elusive and seemed concerned only with Jessica's direct pleasure.

Tanya moved down to where Jessica's midriff was exposed between the corset and the panties and planted soft, wet kisses there. Jessica shivered. This was far better than she could have hoped for.

The salesgirl pulled the panties down over Jessica's hips and to her knees, then went back to kissing the exposed skin. With her hands on both of

Jessica's hips, Tanya kissed Jessica's clitoris, then started licking Jessica's vulva and clitoris, in long, broad strokes.

Jessica gasped with pleasure. Tanya kept licking and inserted two fingers into Jessica's pussy. Jessica gasped again, and moaned so loudly, Tanya put her free hand over Jessica's mouth.

They both froze when they heard a noise outside the curtain. "Is everything okay in there?" said a voice.

"My manager," Tanya mouthed silently.

Jessica nodded and Tanya removed her hand. "Yes," Jessica said. "Just having a bit of trouble with the hooks on this corset."

"Do you need help?" the voice asked. "I've got a salesgirl in here already," Jessica said. "Tanya."

"Okay," the voice said. "Let me know if you need any more help."

"I will," Jessica said. They heard the woman walk away and then both took a collective deep breath. Tanya started licking Jessica's clit again right away.

The thought of being caught mixed with the surprise of being entangled like this at all made Jessica hotter than she thought possible. Tanya grabbed one of Jessica's breasts and started kneading it while she focused her tongue on Jessica's clitoris, flicking back and forth, faster, and faster.

Jessica couldn't take it anymore. She inhaled sharply and felt her orgasm coming. Tanya noticed and put her hand back over Jessica's mouth. Tanya didn't stop licking Jessica's clitoris, and her fingers found Jessica's G-spot.

Jessica moaned as loud as she could through Tanya's hand as she felt her body submit to the orgasm. Electricity shot through her thighs and back as she came again and again. Tanya held her face up and watched, her thumb rubbing Jessica's clit lightly, two fingers still inside Jessica's pussy.

When Jessica was done moaning, Tanya lifted her hand off Jessica's mouth.

"Oh my God," Jessica said. "I need to go lingerie shopping more often."

Tanya smiled. Jessica smiled back. They examined each other for a moment.

"So," Jessica said. "When do you get off?"

Tanya's smile broadened. "Whenever you're ready to help me."

Jessica laughed.

Made in the USA
Columbia, SC
08 October 2023